Genesis Beach

Susan Whitfield

Cover by Linda Houle

*Genesis Beach is dedicated to my husband, Doyle,
the beacon of my life.*

Acknowledgements

The Cape Lookout Lighthouse beacon swished by every fifteen seconds, emitting thoughts of those who were inspirational to me as I wrote Genesis Beach, my first novel.

Thanks, Robbie Whitman, for the unusual murder weapon, and for being my law enforcement resource.

Thank you, Robin Smith, for professional editing, guidance, and encouragement.

Tremendous gratitude, Gladys Prince, for untold hours of editing with lethal but patient attention to detail, and especially for years of unconditional friendship and support.

Thank you, Mary Daly, for sharing my curiosity for bizarre research, for joining me on inspirational trips, for hours of technical assistance, and for unwavering friendship.

Above all, thank you, my family—Doyle, Heath, Graham, Kim, and Crystal—for encouraging my passion for writing and enduring many speculative scene readings.

1

Shit! Five minutes late. The chief would be pissed. I swung the office door open and greeted Maggie York, the dispatcher, with a big smile. I didn't see Charlie Weiss, the Genesis Beach Chief of Police, or Max Cash, his only officer.

"Good morning, Maggie. Sorry I'm late." I looked forward to hearing her respond in that wonderful Ocracoke brogue each day.

"Oh, don't worry abuit it Logan. Charlie's on tha phone in his office and Max is in there too. Some woman called auit of her wit about something roight before you came in, so don't get comfy. You'll be heading roight back auit tha door." She lifted a biscuit toward me. "Take this biscuit. You need some meat on your bone."

"Oh, I couldn't take your biscuit."

"Please. Do me a fava. Oi already ate one," she confessed.

"You're a doll, Maggie. Thanks." I seized the warm soft fluffy biscuit breakfast, wiping drool from my chin. As I took my first bite, Charlie's door burst open and he walked toward the door with Max following close behind.

"Let's go, Logan," the chief bellowed in a troubled voice. I gave Maggie a glance and shrugged as I took off after them, still clinging to the biscuit. Charlie looked over his shoulder as I rushed in the direction of his cruiser. Apparently I'd have to wait to find out what was going on.

"Follow us in your car, Logan. I'll fill you in when we get there."

Without a word I ran to my ten-year-old BMW and jumped in, hoping it would start so I could catch the speeding police car.

Grunt. Grind. Sputter.

Without thinking about the biscuit in my hand, I banged my fist on the dashboard. "Come on, you piece of shit! This is no time to let me down!" I uncurled my fist at the mess I'd made of my breakfast, snatched a napkin out of my console, and wiped cheese from between my fingers.

"Come on, damn it!" The old car obliged after all and I spurted off, not having enough information to know exactly where Charlie and Max went.

As I raced past TideLand, the only mansion on the beach, I saw cruiser lights at the top of the hill. I slammed on brakes and did a doughnut, kicking up sand as I swished the edge of pavement with my tires.

TideLand was the estate of pool and spa mogul Rick Teater, a North Carolina boy who'd built his empire from scratch, and I'd heard rumors about how he chose to spend his fortune. Somebody had probably tried to rob him. The private estate perched above the Atlantic Ocean a considerable distance from any other developed property could be a lucrative target for thieves.

Charlie and Max headed through a side entrance while I screeched up and hopped out. Charlie said Teater's maid called, screaming hysterically that she'd found Rick Teater unresponsive in the hot tub. As we entered the mansion, I began looking for details of a suspicious nature. I scanned floors and walls for any sign of blood even though I had no idea what happened. We passed several rooms, including a colossal kitchen, where I slowed my pace momentarily, then caught up with Charlie and Max who had arrived at the hub of activity in a large, completely enclosed room. An in-home spa, I supposed.

Howie Hurt, the county coroner, and an upset Asian maid stood over the body of Rick Teater still in the tub, on high speed, with white froth lapping out onto gold marble floor. White embroidered towels draped over the tub's heated bar hadn't been touched.

The maid walked away and sat on a nearby bench, wiping her tears. The tub began emitting a sound similar to an S-O-S. Charlie kneeled down and switched it off. Rick Teater, a good-looking man with a blond receding hairline, dark tan, and a pierced left nipple, was in great shape…for a dead man.

"Howie, it's been a long time." I stuck out a hand. He gave me the once over.

"Logan? Logan Hunter? I can't believe it. You're a police officer?"

"Better than that," Charlie responded, touching my arm. "She's SBI."

"Actually I'm interning."

"Man, that's great Logan. You can't be more than twelve." We all laughed.

"Mid-twenties, but thanks," I smiled. "How'd you get here so fast?"

"I live across the highway and two houses down. I heard the maid screaming in the yard and ran over. She's all to pieces. I've got to go back and get my kit. I haven't touched him."

"I have a PERK in the car. I'll get it too," I said. A Physical Evidence Recovery Kit is a mandate for every agent to keep at all times. Unfortunately the SBI didn't issue interns a state-owned car to go with it. In small towns, responsibility for gathering trace evidence usually fell to local police or the closest agent. At least we had a coroner and Howie had attended the same high school I did although six grades ahead of me.

I'd started my SBI internship at Genesis Beach Police Department by default. Just before my start date in Greenville, my mother—considerably older than all my friends' mothers—had a stroke. Rather than drop out of the program altogether, I requested assignment with Charlie at Genesis P.D. It made sense. I had to complete at minimum of four hundred hours of community service to get college credit, and Mother lived on the beach, an island shaped like a slingshot, off Carolina's Crystal Coast.

For two weeks there had been little to do at the station, so I reconnected with a few of my old high school buddies when I could, and spent as much time as possible with my mother at night. I found an old chum tending bar on the beach and gal pals who stayed around after graduation. Sue Hope taught school, Marcia Baker worked at a law enforcement office on the mainland, and Barbara Rivenbark opened her own tavern and grill called Tootsie's. They ribbed me about becoming an agent when I'd usually been the one to lead the pack into mischief in school.

My biggest assignment so far: riding up and down the beach a couple of times a day, checking doors on vacant homes and businesses, passing the marina to make sure all yachts and boats were secured, and going for pizza or subs for two policemen and Maggie, who ate constantly and was called Genesis Beach Carb Queen behind her back.

Mother recovered rapidly and decided to move to Wilmington permanently to be near an older best friend in a retirement home, leaving me with the old beach house. She moved few of the hundreds of oil paintings she'd accomplished over the years, taking her favorites to display on her small studio apartment walls. The rest of her collection stayed in the house along with many memories of my childhood with my parents. I'd taken Daddy's old fly rod off the wall my first night and polished it before placing it back on its hooks, and I'd wound his antique Atlantic Coastline Railroad depot clock. I enjoyed the quiet relaxed pace of the beach again, soothed by the clock's dependable tick-tock. That is, until this morning.

I brought in my PERK and got out gloves for Charlie, Max, and me. Charlie finished giving instructions to Max to get a complete statement from the maid. He turned to me, running his hand through his substantial hair. "On the surface this looks pretty cut and dried. But Howie looks puzzled, and I don't think he buys natural causes."

I moved around near the body and knelt beside it, not looking directly at Rick Teater's face. "Any ideas, Charlie?"

"No." He walked over and put his hand on my shoulder, motioning me out onto the adjacent patio away from the others. "Logan, I want this place searched from roof to basement. Yard, beach. Everything. Just in case he didn't die by himself. I'm in charge, of course, but you have the training to see things Max and I might miss. We're not very experienced with murder around here."

And I am?

2

The only people I see are fishing way down the beach," said Max as we worked our way around the immense stucco mansion, following a gold-colored walk to the Infinity pool, which gave the illusion its water was part of the ocean itself. I looked around the huge pool area and headed toward the gazebo where Max went, stopping to notice its bright-red pitched roof adorned with a whale weather vane, whirling furiously, as if to alert us something was wrong.

A path of wood planks flanked by two rows of warped pine trees led down to the beach. I scooted down the path to sand and looked around. I didn't know what to look for. I didn't see any tracks, footprints, or people anywhere in the vicinity.

"I don't see anything," I shouted at Max. "Besides, we don't know somebody offed him."

"True enough," Max responded. "Could be natural causes."

We climbed back up the hill and maneuvered around several fuchsia crepe myrtle bushes. I proceeded to the front doors, constructed of heavy wood with clear leaded-glass insets. I stepped into the blue slate foyer and moved toward shaggy white rugs, remembering to check my shoes for beach sand. I'd never been inside a house of this magnitude until today. I looked back for Max, but he'd headed toward the garage.

A mammoth whitewashed stone fireplace directed me some twenty-five yards across the vaulted living room where an unframed picture overflowed with vibrant hues of cobalt blue, turquoise, and lemon yellow. A leather couch positioned to take advantage of the panoramic ocean view caught my eye. Across from it, two upholstered chairs in stunning sherbet colors snuggled between many live plants in stone pots.

I stuck my head into an immaculate green bedroom where everything appeared to be in order. I peered into the enormous kitchen that looked like it belonged in a swanky restaurant, as vibrant as other rooms with the addition of large amounts of stainless steel, plenty of light from windows, and two skylights, no doubt built for professional chefs. I walked in to get a better look.

Worktables were massive stainless fixtures with jute rope baskets underneath, full of kitchen gadgets. I looked over tables at stainless steel pot racks barely within arm's reach, but not many pots and pans hooked on. As I looked down I noticed the pumpkin gold marble floor had deep scratches near the refrigerator.

"I'm nervous about this case." Charlie leaned on doorframe. "The SBI will probably want to get involved. We don't have this kind of trouble here. I'm not sure I want them traipsing in here and taking over," he walked over to the scratches. "Um, wouldn't think Teater would have this. They look like new scratches too." He straightened. "I liked Rick Teater. I don't understand what happened here. He's never been sick that I know of. What do you think?" Charlie asked, looking me dead in the eyes.

"Well, from what I understand, Rick Teater lived life at racetrack speed. He's rumored to be a heavy boozer and a wild partier—drugs and lots of sex. I don't know if any of it's true. Maybe he overdosed on drugs or had a heart attack, or maybe he pissed on somebody."

"Yeah, you're right. Even though I liked the man, he had a past that's bound to include enemies. He made a few building his empire, I'm sure. And lots of women might not have understood his need for variety."

Charlie set his jaw. His thick salt-and-pepper hair made him seem wise and experienced, but he was more nervous than I'd ever seen him. His nose made him hard to look at straight on. It resembled a large bruised Red Delicious apple with stiff bristles coming from it. I'd never seen Charlie drink but had to wonder if he was a lush off duty. I'd witnessed his sinus and allergy problems, though, so that might be the reason his nose stayed bulbous and ruddy. His nervousness made it throb.

"Seriously, Logan, you know Max and I don't have any experience with murder, if that's what it turns out to be. We're going to need lots of help from you," Charlie concluded.

"I'll be glad to do all I can, but you realize I'm an intern. I've never actually worked a homicide, just textbook scenarios. Charlie, you're in charge. I think it's your call whether the SBI comes in or not. They wouldn't get involved just because I'm interning here. You'd have to ask for help. If we do all the investigating ourselves, we'll have to rope this place off and keep everyone out to maintain the integrity of the scene. I'll use my evidence kit and be as thorough as possible. If that's not enough, we can always ask for state help. And what about your brother? Can you check with him without making it an official request?"

"My brother and I aren't that close. I'd rather not open a door for him." I didn't quite understand his hesitation but didn't push the issue.

"Well, we're jumping the gun anyhow. We don't even know for sure it's a homicide. Teater may have had health issues nobody knew about. At any rate, his death will hit papers and TV stations today. You'll have to make a statement."

"Oh, yeah, Maggie just patched me that four TV stations have already called asking about foul play."

"Let's not tell them anything other than that Rick Teater is dead." Charlie nodded agreement. I walked over to Howie, writing notes in his journal. His evidence containers sat at his feet.

"Howie. Can you tell me how he died?"

Howie bit the ink pen for a second before responding. "It's difficult to say at this point without doing an autopsy, but I find it hard to believe he died in this tub. His skin doesn't look right. If he drowned, he wouldn't have been sitting up. If he had a heart attack, he wouldn't be this color, unless he'd been here for a long time. And he looked like he'd been propped up. The maid said she never touched him. No, I can't confirm anything yet, Logan. I'll get back to you as soon as I can. I'll work through the night if I have to."

"How soon will you be through here?"

"I'm leaving with the body in a few minutes. The wagon's on the way. The maid says there's no family. I'll get you a copy of my report as soon as I can, and I'll call if something comes up you need to know. You have plenty to do here with little help. One disadvantage of a small town investigation. Get any evidence you find to me as fast as you can," Howie advised. I glanced at the zipped body bag.

"Will do."

"Howie, if you live across the street, I guess you knew him?"

"No, not really. I work the whole county and have little time for socializing. He didn't run with the same crowd I did. Kind of aloof, if you want my honest opinion. I don't play golf so I never ran into him. He didn't do anything outside; he hired gardeners and yard people to handle all that."

"I'll make a note to talk with all of them if this turns out to be a homicide."

I hurried away to check out the back of the property more thoroughly. The hot tub inside the covered patio area wasn't like any patio I'd ever seen. On one side, a surprisingly pink stucco wall had a simple gray wood bench running its length, above it dozens of parchment prints of dried ocean or beach flora protected by glare-proof glass.

A tall weathered arbor beckoned me to the pool. About the time I cleared the arbor, water spurting from both sides startled me. I noticed enough transplanted palm trees flanking both sides of the pool to provide plenty of privacy even though there were no other houses near Teater's private paradise.

I walked to the end of the pool and turned back around toward the two-story mansion. An expansive balcony adjacent to what appeared to be a vaulted master suite caught my attention—high enough to give the millionaire an uncluttered view of the ocean both night and day. Rick Teater's love nest. *Nice.* I'd look around more closely once the others left. There might be clues to what happened up there.

As I walked around the edge of the pool, I noticed some dried muddy footprints. I stooped to get a closer look and pulled my magnifying glass out of my suit pocket to make sure I saw straight. I pushed back a short blonde piece of hair and rearranged my wire-framed glasses. The print on one foot appeared to be missing a part of the big toe. I reached for my PDA, snapped a digital picture of both footprints, and input its location. I called out to the chief, peeking around the corner.

"Hey, Charlie, was Rick Teater missing a toe?"

"Not that I'm aware of. Why?" he asked, walking over to me. I showed him the footprint.

"Somebody's definitely been here. We need to find out who's missing a toe and ask some questions."

"It could be the pool guy, I suppose, but I'll call Howie to check Teater's feet," he promised, taking the bright yellow crime tape out of his pocket.

The adrenalin jolted through my veins like I'd been plugged into an electrical outlet. My heart skipped at launching my first investigation.

What if it is murder? Am I ready for this?

I thought back to how I'd prepared for this kind of case. During my senior year of high school, I'd taken Criminal Justice and been intrigued by those who break the law and by those who are the victims.

I completed my Criminal Justice degree at East Carolina University, excelling in every area, but my professors thought I needed work in tactfulness and being a team player. I admit I like to do things on my own, but I learned to be cooperative and share for "the sake of the team". Delighted to be accepted into the North Carolina State Bureau of Investigation intern program—the state's equivalent of the Feds—I was twenty-five—a little older than most interns— six feet, one inch, and wore a size four. Strong and quick for my age and size, I had more stamina than many younger men in the program.

After talking to Howie, I didn't think for one minute Rick Teater died in the hot tub. I'd be delving into everything about him over the next few days. "Max cordoned off the entire estate. There's not supposed to be anybody here now but you, Logan. Let yourself out. I'm going back to the station. Use the radio if you find something, and I'll run back over," Charlie sighed. "I hope we can get the forensics report fast. Oh, by the way, Max interviewed the maid. You may want to check with him before we leave." I walked the chief toward the front door and headed over to Max.

He closed his notebook as I approached. "Max, did you find out anything from the maid?"

"She has a heavy Asian accent—choppy and hard to follow in between her sobs. She said she'd known Mr. Teater for years, and her husband worked for him in Japan. She said they were highly respected in Japan, and Teater treated them well. He even hired her husband to run his company over there. He died, and Teater offered to bring her to America. She's looked after Teater and kept house for him ever since. She's pretty torn up about finding him. She wasn't aware of any enemies though, not even his old girlfriends."

3

After I walked back through the mansion and around the pool again, I dug my running shoes out of the car, stretched, and had run five miles when I noticed a woman running frantically toward the Teater mansion. Not jogging. All out running, flailing her arms, and making strangling sobbing sounds.

"O...Oh... my G...God!" The woman dipped under the crime tape, puffing hard but apparently pumped with adrenalin. Once she caught her breath, she completed the ascent to the gazebo. She stopped and bent over, putting her hands on her knees, coiling her body into a crescent, trying to catch her breath, and crying all at once.

Having stayed around to see if anyone showed up, I glided up behind her and grabbed her arm, surprising her. "Can I help you?" I shouted. "You can't be here jeopardizing the crime scene."

The woman, still out of breath, shook her head and tried to wipe away the tears that wouldn't stop. She reached for my arm. "No, I have to see Rick...I—"

"Miss, Mr. Teater isn't here. And you have to leave now!" I pointed back down the path.

The woman put the palm of her hand on her heaving chest. "I have to see him; he can't be dead. The news has to be wrong!" The distraught woman sat down on the gazebo steps and wept. I stared for a minute, sizing up the situation, and then sat down near the woman to wait for her to calm down.

She turned to me, fumbling her words. "My name is Pepper Ellis. I…I'm Rick's chef." She blew her nose and gave me a perplexed look.

"I'm Logan Hunter. SBI. I'm working at the Genesis Beach Police Department. May I ask you some questions?" I displayed my intern badge.

"No, I can't deal with this. I can't… Tell me he's all right," she pleaded and began to sob again when I hesitated.

"I'm sorry, Miss Ellis. He's not all right. Where do you live, ma'am?"

The woman pointed down the beach, weeping uncontrollably again.

"What happened to Rick?"

"We don't know yet."

"But he's…dead?"

"I'm afraid so, ma'am."

Once the wails softened to whimpers, she looked at me with bloodshot eyes, blinking at lightning speed. "I walked, no, I ran here from my house. It's not far. I don't live on the beach…a few blocks over. But I ran to the beach and kept running until I got here. I saw it on the news." She seized my arm, her Carolina blue eyes penetrating mine. "Please tell me what happened. Where is he? Is he still here? Oh, please let me go to him."

I waited again for her to calm down. "No, I've already told you he isn't here. Look, I'm finished for a while. Let me walk you home since you're so upset."

She stood, not trying to go beyond the gazebo. She glanced over her shoulder a couple of times as we walked the path back down to the beach. I held on to her arm to keep her from falling. "I live down the beach that way, near the country club," she directed, almost in a whisper.

We walked in silence for over a mile before Pepper Ellis pointed up to a sand dune. We crawled over the soft sand. I was wearing running shoes, and she still had Enzos in her hand, finally dropping them, and sliding her feet into them. We walked across two roads and angled up a paved path until she stopped in front of a condo.

"This is it."

"Will you be all right by yourself?"

She met my line of vision and sighed. "Can you come in for a few minutes? I guess I need to explain a few things," Pepper murmured, wiping her nose.

"I'll come in for a few minutes if you're sure you're up to it," I said.

The gray condominium sat near many others similar to it on the sound. It had been landscaped around the front entrance. A gleaming black Fiat was parked nearby. I could see the marina about six blocks south where the sound divided the two strips of the island into a slingshot.

Pepper Ellis walked up the steps almost in a trance and tried to unlock the door.

"Well, I guess I didn't lock up."

As I walked inside, I observed a creamy white living room with a ten-foot ceiling of gorgeous stained wood. The fireplace, bordered by overflowing bookshelves probably meant this was a year-round home. A glance at book titles revealed that almost all were about the culinary arts. A framed pen-and-ink picture of a young girl in a gingham skirt with a kerchief on her head leaned on the mantel. The young girl resembled Pepper Ellis.

A wing chair sat nearby with a leather footstool that didn't seem to match the couch in red stripes. A fabric-covered table held several magazines, and behind it a sofa table covered in burlap held a brown spindle lamp, an array of seashells, and several pairs of sunglasses. The chef switched on the lamp and disappeared into the kitchen.

"Damn!" I heard her say.

"Don't go to any trouble. I just wanted to make sure you got home safely." When I didn't get a response, I walked to the kitchen door where the strong smell of Prosecco curled through my nostrils. Picking up shards of glass, she pointed me toward a closet. I returned with a broom, a dustpan, and a mop.

"I was making Sangria when I heard the news on Channel 3," Pepper explained. I remained silent while she sobbed, trying to catch her breath and arrest the shock and pain. Once we finished cleaning up the mess, she went to a cabinet, pulled out two wine flutes, and filled both with a beautiful dark purple liquid.

She settled into the couch, set her own wine glass on the fabric coffee table, and put her hands over her eyes. "Please sit down," she said motioning, to the white chair. I sat and sipped the wine, smelled it, and drank more, even though I wasn't supposed to drink on duty. I glanced at my watch. But technically I was off duty for the day, if an agent ever is off duty.

"Thank you. This is delicious wine. I've never had any quite like it." I studied the wine and the woman, and waited for her to begin the explanation she'd promised.

"Um, it's homemade. The wine? I make my own. Briar berry is great for tummy problems or indigestion, which I've had a lot of the past few hours." I drank up. She bowed her head and began to cry, her shoulders shaking as she sobbed. After a few minutes she composed herself.

"I'm a chef. I graduated from the College of Culinary Arts at Johnson and Wales University in Charleston. Rick hired me from a mediocre job in Wilmington. I've been cooking for him for about two years. He likes…um, liked...to entertain, so I came up with something creative and delicious for as many as one hundred of his guests at a time. I planned to save money to open my own restaurant where every item on the menu is an original creation." The smile that had crept across her face suddenly disappeared. "I can't believe he's d...dead." She began to cry again, and I kept quiet. A few minutes passed.

"Miss Ellis, did Mr. Teater have any health problems?"

"Not that I'm aware of. I mean, he did drink and use drugs at one time, but that was before I met him. He never took medicine, so I don't think he had any problems." She twisted and snatched up a couch cushion.

"As I'm sure you'll find out, Agent Hunter, I was more than Rick's chef. I have more clothes there than I do here. Pretty much a live-in chef. We became lovers," she sniffled and snatched a tissue from a box on the floor, calming herself.

"We became lovers about a year ago. Oh, I knew about his reputation, and the other women. In fact, I cooked for Rick and his dates in the early months. One night his date called and cancelled after I'd started an extravagant meal. He said he enjoyed watching me cook, and he wanted me to finish the meal and be his date. I felt a little uncomfortable, dressed to cook, not for a date, and certainly not with Rick Teater. His women wore skimpy, sexy clothes, and most were younger than I am.

"Anyway, that began something special, or at least I thought so until last night. He'd stopped seeing other women as far as I know, and spent almost every evening with me. Or I should say, I spent almost every night with him." Pepper Ellis smiled for an instant and then looked miserable.

"What happened last night?"

"Well, yesterday morning I told Rick I needed to come home and take care of some things, and I'd go back and cook us a late dinner. He planned to play golf and wouldn't want to eat early anyway. I didn't know that would be the last time I saw him." She began to wail, getting off the couch, and pacing the floor. I sat still, not yet willing to leave, but feeling awkward.

She blew her nose. "It took me longer than I expected to handle some business and run some errands. I went by the market and got to Rick's about eight.

"I have my own key so I let myself in. I went straight to the kitchen and called out to him I was sorry about being so late. I marinated some steaks and went to find him. I knew he was home, because he had left his golf clubs out to clean. I figured he was in the shower, so I headed upstairs to the master suite." The chef cleared her throat, choking back more tears.

"I opened the bedroom door," she paused, "and saw him on the bed with Chyna, a hooker from down the beach."

"Wait! Wait!" I shouted, stopping her. "You can't talk to me anymore. You need to call a lawyer."

She jumped off the couch. "What are you talking about? Why? What are you saying?" She ran over to me and grabbed my arm. "What the hell are you saying?"

"Listen to me. What you told me makes you a prime suspect if this turns out to be a homicide. You're his lover. You found him in bed with another woman. Motive. Don't you understand? You had a motive to kill him!" I looked into her wet eyes, already wishing I'd handled the situation with more finesse.

The chef pointed to the door. "You need to leave. Now! Get the hell out of my house!"

She slammed the door behind me, and I still could hear the wails until I was on the beach near the breakers. My tact had abandoned me.

I'd have to do some serious damage control if I expected to get anywhere with this case. I headed back up the beach, kicking sand and cursing myself.

4

The nightmare was intense. I never remembered much detail, but I understood someone reaching for me with long bony fingers and horrifyingly long nails terrified me. I had that recurring nightmare when tense, excited, or worried. It had been happening off and on for years but now occurred much more frequently.

In the beginning I only knew sketchy details upset me. Gradually the fingers emerged with the long nails. After this week's events, I knew the nightmare would return. Excitement about the Teater case unsettled my nerves. I couldn't get the events of the past twenty-four hours out of my mind: dead millionaire, hooker, and a girlfriend with motive and opportunity.

I needed to talk to Charlie, and find this Chyna and talk to her. And I definitely would see Pepper Ellis again. I couldn't believe how badly I'd handled her.

The left footprint with part of the big toe missing intrigued me too. I got my PDA out of my jacket and looked at the digital pictures I'd taken earlier, the first one the weird left footprint by the pool. I zoomed in on it and studied it for a minute. I compared it to the right footprint, and they seemed identical, except for the big toe. These prints might prove Rick Teater had another visitor the night he died. Unless Chyna had a deformed toe.

I walked to the kitchen and heard Lexus, my Himalayan, meowing as she came to greet me. Hungry, I'm sure. I hadn't even thought about feeding her. I poured some Deli-Cat and scratched her ears before throwing on some shorts and a tee for my morning run. Once I returned, I grabbed a chilled Starbuck's Frappuccino from the refrigerator, guzzling half of it on the way to the shower. I wanted to be over at the estate before any other officers arrived to check out Teater's bedroom where the chef said she found him with Chyna, the hooker.

5

As I pulled my old Beemer into the paved drive, an impressive brass TideLand sign greeted me. I sighed. I didn't come early enough; officers and camera crews were already outside. Max waved me through with his terminally pale freckled arm.

"I see you got the fun detail," I teased.

"Yes, but Charlie's not looking forward to making a statement to the media. I'd rather be doing this," Max replied, running his hand through his carroty hair. "He's inside grumbling."

I parked as close to the front door as I could, grabbed the evidence kit from the back seat, and went inside. I saw Charlie across the room, talking to some lab techs. Dressed in a dark suit with white shirt and conservative tie, the chief of police looked anxious, which made his large red nose more prominent; I figured it would show up well on camera. I waved and walked over.

"You clean up nice."

"Thanks, kid. I know I'm just ravishing. Did you find anything else interesting after I left?" wheezed Charlie, battling a bronchial infection. He blew his apple nose into a tattered handkerchief and pushed it into his pocket.

"Just the footprints. Oh, yeah, and a visitor, his chef and live-in girlfriend, Pepper Ellis, either torn up about it or a good actress. I want to check out the master suite. She claims she walked in on Teater and a Chyna somebody—a hooker—and then gathered up her things and left. If that's true, Pepper Ellis had a motive. But Chyna may have been the last to see him alive. She could've killed him."

"That would be Chyna Neary. I know her. And that's a very interesting tidbit. Nothing's ever cut and dried, is it? I guess that's why we need investigators like you." He looked around, pulling at his shirt collar. "I swear I hate talking to the media. They'll try to make me say things I don't want to say. Hell, I don't know anything. We're still not positive it's murder."

"No, not really. I guess I'm getting ahead of myself with my theory about what happened."

Charlie looked out the window, straightened his tie, and smoothed his thick hair. "I can only tell them he's dead and we're investigating. Be back in a minute." Charlie headed for the front door, moaning and scratching his ass as he went. I hated it for him but was glad I didn't have to face them. I made a note in my PDA that Chyna's last name was Neary, and headed upstairs to the master bedroom.

The door was ajar; I pushed it with a gloved hand. The master suite was in scale with the rest of the mansion—vaulted ceiling, dramatic wall color somewhere between olive and emerald. In the middle of the bay window a metal floor lamp monkey pointed out into the Atlantic Ocean. A dark rattan chair sat near the foot of the bed.

The king-sized bed had wood and brass posts supporting the massive mirror that ran its full length. I walked around it, observing linens in good shape after a night of wild sex, if Pepper Ellis told the truth. Pillow shams were out of place but the comforter was only a little rumpled, making it easy for me to spot a few stains near the headboard. I called to Max, who had moved inside while Charlie placated reporters.

"Hey, Max, did somebody make this bed?"

"No, I'm sure we haven't let anybody in this room."

"It's odd that it's in such good shape, based on the chef's statement." I opened the kit and retrieved a swab and plastic evidence bag. I collected some of the dried stain and sealed the bag before labeling it and writing my initials. Semen or something else? I noticed a dirty wine goblet on the nightstand. It appeared to have thick residue in it. I swabbed some of the residue into another baggie, sealed it, and labeled it. I pulled out my PDA and clicked pictures from every angle of the bed, the stains, and the goblet. The process would continue with everything I thought might be evidence of what really happened to Teater.

As Max reached for the goblet with an ungloved hand, I grabbed his wrist. "Max! Where are your gloves? Don't touch anything without them. You could be destroying evidence. We have to do this the right way. If Howie calls it homicide, do you want your fingerprints to compromise everything?"

Max scratched his head, turned cherry red, and reached into my kit for another pair of gloves, apologizing. "How stupid can I be?" I'd embarrassed him, but I suppose he'd never had to use gloves in this small beach town. Max held a bag while I lifted the goblet between my fingertips so prints wouldn't be disturbed. He sealed the bag, and I labeled it.

I made my way to the master bathroom, opened the shower door, and took a picture. No bar soap, not in the shower or in the soap dishes on the vanities. No liquid soap or shower gel anywhere either. I made a note in case this meant something. Surely the man washed with some kind of soap.

I opened a linen closet and saw three rounds of expensive bath soap on the shelf. With a freshly gloved hand, I lifted the lid on a fancy round silver box of Cor. Four more rounds. I'd heard of this soap made with flecks of real silver. *Bet that extravagance set him back a pretty penny.* I photographed them. But did Teater start with fresh soap every day?

I was about to leave the master suite when my eye caught an object outside the bathroom door: a man's cotton sock, a tube sock with a red stripe. I found it odd Rick Teater would wear this kind of cheap sock. It just didn't fit. In the few pictures I'd seen of him, he wore no socks at all. I picked it up with my large tweezers, and bagged and labeled the dirty sock.

"A tube sock. It may be nothing, but a cheap sock in this place just seems out of place."

"I've never noticed Mr. Teater wearing socks of any kind," Max said. "Most of the beach folks don't wear any socks at all unless it's for church." He left with the two pieces of possible evidence.

I walked downstairs, headed for the pool area, and glanced at the footprint again. It was beginning to look like rain, so I didn't want to wait any longer to double-check the sand. I had a picture of this print in case it washed away.

I followed the wooden walk past the gazebo, noticing the motionless whale weathervane. I went on down the hill to the beach, looking as closely as I could at the sand near the steps where someone might have decided to go up. It had an odd look, like it had been combed—or raked.

As I ambled a little farther north, I spotted something in a large clump of seaweed—a rake, the kind golf courses use in their bunkers to rake out tracks for the next golfer. I took a picture before I picked up the rake with my gloved hand.

I concluded the rake had been used to wipe out tracks. I used the rake to pull seaweed apart, still looking for more clues. And there it was: a beautiful footprint missing part of the big toe, a perfect match to the print by the pool. I clicked several digital pictures before I grabbed the rake and ran up the path. Charlie came around the gazebo with sweat pouring from his face as I reached him.

"Charlie, look what I found." We sat down under the gazebo and examined the rake. I explained the other track and that I'd taken pictures of the location of the rake and other footprints. "We need to pour some plaster in it so we can have it for extra evidence to go with my picture."

Charlie scratched his head. "We don't have any plaster."

"There's some mix in the trunk of my Beemer," I explained.

"Plaster, huh? Top priority," ordered Charlie, looking up at Max as he approached us.

"I'm on it," responded Max, running back toward the driveway.

"Oh, Logan, Howie called. He said there's no doubt Rick Teater was murdered, but he's not sure how yet," Charlie said softly, wiping his brow.

I told Charlie the bedroom scene bugged me. I would have to question Pepper Ellis again, and certainly Chyna Neary, when I located her.

"I need to talk to the maid too. What's her name again?"

"Akiko Higushi, or something like that. Terribly upset, and there's no reason to suspect her. She worked for him at least six years. Very loyal, I understand.

"I want to ask her some questions. After all, she found him."

Charlie nodded. "She ought to be fairly easy to find. I'll check into where she lives. I heard her husband ran Teater's Japanese interests until his death, and I think he's looked after her since then."

"What happened to the husband?"

"I don't really know. I just remember hearing years ago that Teater brought her here since she was in financial trouble and he wanted to help her. Rick was generous with lots of folks. That's why it's so hard to think anybody would want to kill him."

"Well, now we have to find a murderer. This internship's turned out to be a humdinger."

"Yep," the chief said, "and at least we're ahead of the game by being proactive."

6

Pepper Ellis, unhappy to see me standing at her door, tried to slam it, but I managed to get my foot inside and stop the force of the door from knocking me down the front steps. The pain in my ankle reverberated all the way to my head. *Damn, that hurt!*

"Go away. I don't want you here!" she screamed. "How dare you come back!" I put my hands in the air and tried to remain calm. I'd learned staying calm although I felt like lashing out at her and charging her with assaulting a law enforcement officer. But, hey! I'd caused this reaction so I checked my temper, the best tactic under these circumstances. The hands in the air represented a truce on my part but not a sign of weakness.

"That wasn't necessary, Ms. Ellis. I'm investigating a murder. I could haul you in for injuring a law enforcement agent and obstructing this investigation," I managed to squeak out, "I need to ask you some more questions." No response.

"I was only trying to protect you by not letting you tell me too much without a lawyer. I didn't mean to imply you killed Rick Teater. But I *do* think you can help catch his killer."

The chef, who had retreated deeper into the living room, turned as I limped into the room. "How?"

"By answering a few questions honestly."

"No, I mean, how did Rick die?"

"I can't give you any details on that, Miss Ellis. We're still trying to fit the pieces together."

I hoped to avoid any more tantrums that might injure me. Her red, moist eyes looked away, but she nodded. I closed the front door, rubbed my traumatized ankle, and limped to the white chair since she was back on the striped couch, looking dazed.

"Look, I know this is terrible for you, but I need some help. I've been back to Tideland this morning. I found a couple of interesting things. Maybe you can shed some light on them. Would you be willing to help me work through them?"

She shifted on the couch, grabbing a cushion and holding it under her chin. "But don't you think I killed him? Didn't you say it had to be me because I caught Rick in bed with that hooker?"

I sat up and looked her straight in the eyes. "No, Ms. Ellis. That's not what I said at all. Actually this hooker may have been the last person with him. But your story doesn't add up. I checked the master bedroom myself and there's no evidence of wild sex going on. Or any sex for that matter. The bedding was hardly rumpled. I got the report from the lab that tested all the bed linens, including the comforter, and there were no body fluids on anything, so I don't see how they could've been having sex when you saw them."

The chef tossed the cushion aside and sat up, staring at me. "But I *saw* them. Is this some kind of trick? I saw Chyna on top of Rick." The distraught woman was on her feet, pointing her finger at me while she paced back and forth between the sofa and the chair I sat in.

"Let's back up a minute. Maybe what you thought you saw isn't really what you saw. Emotions have a way of distorting things. I need you to think carefully before you answer. I'm not here to hurt you, Miss Ellis, but I can't totally discount you as a suspect without filling in some missing pieces." She nodded, pulling her long hair back with both hands and dropping it between her shoulder blades.

"Start at the beginning, and tell me exactly what you did after you picked up steaks at the market and headed to Mr. Teater's."

"Okay, I had my own key so I let myself in. Rick was home because he always left his golf clubs out to clean before he put them up. He was immaculate about everything. Anyway, I went straight to the kitchen with my groceries and called out that I was back. Of course, the place is huge, so if he were in the shower, he wouldn't hear me. I unwrapped the steaks, put them in a dish, and poured some of my special marinade on them and went upstairs to look for him—like I already told you. I assumed he was in the shower, so I opened the bedroom door and was about to step into the room when I saw Chyna straddling Rick—"

"Okay, stop for a minute. Explain in detail how Rick looked and how Chyna looked. I'm not trying to cause you more pain, but this is critically important." The chef swallowed hard and reached for a tissue. After wiping her eyes, she continued. "As I said, Chyna was on top—"

"Okay," I waved my hand for her to stop again. "They were both naked? Were they under the covers or on top of the comforter?"

Pepper thought for a moment. "Actually, I couldn't see anything but Rick's feet. They were on top of the comforter because they were across the bed up near the headboard. I totally freaked out! Were they naked? Well, I don't know about Rick since I couldn't see him. Chyna was topless, wearing a T," She shouted at me, jumping off the couch.

"A 'T'?"

"You know, a thong. No, she wasn't completely naked. What does that mean?" Pepper came over to me, maybe thinking I could make her feel better.

"First of all, it seems that if she were wearing a thong and there's no evidence of body fluids on the bed linens or semen from Rick's body, they probably didn't have sex," I concluded. "I mean, it's certainly possible, but there's no evidence to back up that theory."

A puzzled Pepper Ellis sat down on the floor at my feet. "Then what was going on?" she inquired. She suddenly jumped to her feet. "Oh, my God! Was she killing him? Could I have saved him?" Her swollen eyes flashed furiously as she squalled.

"I don't know, but I'm going to find out. I need to talk to this Chyna. Do you know where I can find her? Did she see you? Does she know you saw them?"

"I don't think she ever saw me, and apparently Rick didn't either. I think he would've thrown her off and tried to keep me from leaving. At least, I hope he would have. He was so happy that morning. . .that last morning. He knew I was coming back to make dinner for the two of us. It doesn't make any sense." Her head dropped.

"Chyna's about twenty and built like a brick shit house. She lives somewhere on the beach, but I have no idea where. I've heard she hangs out with a groundskeeper from Genesis Country Golf and Club when she's not getting paid to screw. But I'm not going near her." Pepper snarled, her eyes glistening.

"It's my job to find her, not yours. You've been very helpful. Look, Ms. Ellis, if it's any consolation, I don't think you did it." Giving her my card, I added, "If you hear anything, please call me at this number. If you see this Chyna, don't approach her. Call me."

She grabbed my wrist. "I was in love with him. I realize that now that it's too late. And he loved me too. I'm sure of it. He taught me to swim. I was always afraid of the water. But he was so patient with me. With sex too. I mean patient with my inexperience."

"What did you do after you saw them?"

"I stomped back to the kitchen and started throwing pots and pans." *That would explain the crevices in the floor.* "Then I packed up every pot and pan I owned—even the ones hanging on the racks—and hauled them to my Fiat. They're still in it. I came home and bawled all night."

"We'll get the bastard," I assured her. "I have one more question, though. Did Rick wear striped tube socks?"

"Never! In fact, he seldom wore socks at all. He hated them." She glided across the room as if she were in a trance, stopped, and focused her blue eyes on me.

"I have to find a way to take care of Rick's arrangements. His parents are dead, I think, and he was an only child. I have to take care of him," she finished sadly. Her head jolted up. "Agent Hunter, what if I could have saved Rick? Oh, my God! This is so horrible!" She shrieked hysterically.

I finally calmed her, and I promised to get to the bottom of things. I thanked her for cooperating and quietly let myself out to head for home. The breeze strengthened. I vaguely remembered hearing someone say tropical storm remnants were heading in our direction.

I had a message from Charlie that the lab found spills of an exotic alcohol-based drink on the bedding. Rick's fingerprints were on the goblet from the nightstand along with an unidentified set.

Maybe Pepper Ellis had come in too early. That still didn't account for no evidence of sex later if the couple didn't know the chef had seen them—unless the drink was laced with something lethal. And if it was, and Chyna Neary's fingerprints were on the goblet, she would become the prime murder suspect, and Pepper would be the eyewitness.

Holding a bag of ice on my swollen ankle, I called the lab and asked for as much information as possible about the goblet's contents. You never know what might turn out to be a clue.

Had Chyna put something in Rick's drink? Or had the chef added a lethal ingredient before she left that morning?

7

I went out for the evening dressed in tight jeans and a halter-top. I fastened the strap of my high heel around my purple ankle, but I didn't want to go far enough to attract men looking for a quick pick up. The beachfront throbbed with respectable nightclubs and a lot more seamy taverns and piers. With any luck, I'd run into Chyna Neary.

I started at one end of the beach and worked my way through every sleazy nightclub and tavern I came to. I asked for information about Chyna, and even though some guys knew her, they didn't know where she was, or at least that's what they wanted me to believe.

About one, I walked toward Tramps, a new party spot. As I approached the door, it opened and a young couple came tumbling out, obviously stoned. They bumped into me and laughed with no apology. The girl seemed to stare a hole through me. Her white spandex top left little to the imagination, with strategic nipplage revealing firm perky breasts. I smiled, shook my head, and walked on through the door.

I found a stool at the bar and began idle chitchat with the overweight bartender, who displayed significant butt cleavage when he turned his back to me. I ordered a Long

Island Iced Tea. It arrived and I leaned over and asked him if he'd seen Chyna tonight.

"Yeah, man. She left. You just missed her," answered the bartender. "She left with that dude that works at the golf club."

"What does she look like?"

"Young, messy dark hair, eyes that can see right through you. She's wearing jeans and a white top. He's got hair in his eyes too." I threw a ten-dollar bill on the bar and bolted for the door.

I searched the parking lot, but couldn't find Chyna Neary or the guy she'd wrapped herself around. I'd walked right by Chyna. I had no idea she was so young and so pretty, barely out of her teens. I decided to walk over to the surf to see if the couple was there. Off in the distance I could see them, arm in arm, staggering around on the sand. I pursued from a distance. At least I could find out where she bedded down for the night.

The couple stumbled on for a few hundred yards and headed for the sand dunes, either to make out or to head for home. With heavy clouds and darkness, I could barely see them but followed their giggles as they pulled each other along over the dunes.

They headed for an old wood house not far from Genesis Golf and Country Club. I watched as they disappeared into the old building. Now that I knew what Chyna looked like, I'd find a way to question her. The young man with her must be the one Pepper had mentioned.

I went home and climbed into bed, instantly falling asleep from sheer exhaustion.

8

I awoke on Saturday morning to a yolk peeking through clouds that made it look scrambled. I'd rested well and my ankle had stopped throbbing. No nightmares, thank God.

Looking out on my deck, I could tell it had rained hard, but I hadn't heard it. Now the brightly polished day promised to be a good time to do some more sleuthing. I hadn't eaten much in several days, so I decided to have a bacon and egg sandwich and a cup of strong coffee before heading out the door.

Pepper Ellis came to mind again. I still wasn't sure about her, but my gut told me she didn't do it. Besides, I'd checked out her toes, and she had all of hers. *She could have had an accomplice, but she had easy access to Rick, so why would she need one?* And her hysteria screamed innocence. I had to find out who Rick's real enemies were.

I called Charlie and told him my plan to visit Genesis Golf and Country Club. Maybe I could get a peek at that old building where Chyna and her friend had gone. If he was a groundskeeper, maybe I could observe him from a distance. I decided to pull out my old clubs and set them in the hallway to stick in the car in case I got a chance to hit a few practice swings near the clubhouse.

I stuck some bread in the toaster, fried my bacon, and scrambled two eggs. I wolfed down my sandwich and pulled out some golf shorts, a top with a collar, and some ankle socks, grabbed my Rockports, and poured Lexus enough food and water for the day.

The impressive entrance to Genesis Beach Golf and Country Club screamed money. I would find the pro, Ned Parks, and explain I'd found a sand rake. I'd done my homework. Genesis Golf and Country Club was one of the nicest on North Carolina's Crystal Coast, and the only one perilously close to the surf. The ocean backed several tee boxes, and a number of greens came precariously close to the only barrier between the hole and the water. Thick sea grass and transplanted palm trees like the ones at the Teater mansion, miles down the beach, dotted the immaculate course, throwing sand in fairways and uprooting small trees and bushes.

Charlie had told me there was always a clatter of activity since most Genesis Beach residents were either retired or rich enough to play any time they wanted to. These club members—like Rick Teater—paid large sums of money to maintain the course, a tough assignment on the beach. Constant sea breezes and the occasional nor'easter ate away at the course on a frequent basis, throwing sand on the fairway and downing small trees.

It took hundreds of thousands of dollars to keep the greens plush in this sand. But Charlie said affluent members were willing to pay any price to enjoy the ocean views and relaxed atmosphere away from the mediocre clubs and their mediocre members. Ned Parks had his hands full, keeping the hired help out in the sun and wind constantly in order to appease the rich. He had hired a number of young locals as caddies, and it was most likely the best money they'd ever had. But, according to Charlie, Ned had strict rules about equipment out of place or lost. He had a reputation as a hard liner when it came to a good work ethic and utmost integrity.

Convertibles and expensive SUVs filled the parking lot where I parked my old faded Beemer. I walked up to the Pro Shop desk and asked for Mr. Parks.

"He's back in his office," the lady said, pointing down the hall. She adjusted a large white bow with white flowers on the entrance wall, I assumed in memory of Teater. I walked past many displays of golf balls, golf shirts, and sun visors.

I found the Pro's Office and tapped on the doorframe to get his attention. He looked up and motioned me in, standing up. "Yes? Are you here about the Make A Wish golf tournament?" he asked.

"No, my name is Logan Hunter, Mr. Parks. I'm an SBI intern at the Genesis Beach Police Department. I wanted to come by and see if you were missing a sand rake. I found one on the beach a couple of days ago."

"I'm not aware one's missing," he said.

"I didn't bring it with me, sir, but do you mind if I close the door for a minute so I can explain?"

Ned gave me his full attention.

"I'm sure you've heard about Rick Teater's death."

Ned nodded. "Yes. In fact the flowers are our memorial to him. There wouldn't be golf on Genesis Beach without him. He put up the money for this course, you know. He's the primary investor for this place. I'm the other. I can't believe he's dead. He seemed to be in great health. Rumors are widespread, of course. Some say he had a heart attack and others say he was murdered. I just can't believe anybody'd want to kill him. A great guy," he exclaimed, leaning forward, "to me, anyway. Was he murdered? Was that rake somehow involved?"

"We're still investigating right now, sir, but it is suspicious. I found the rake on the beach at the base of the hill that leads up to Mr. Teater's property. It appears someone used it to cover footprints. The rake's been taken in as possible evidence." That was as much as I'd share with him before the news conference Charlie would conduct later in the day.

"I thought I'd start here and see if the rake was yours. I'm not sure there's any way to tell for sure. There's no brand name or club name on it to indicate who owned it."

Ned scratched his head. "I tell you what I'll do, little lady. I'll find out if it's one of ours. I can probably tell you within the hour if one's missing. I keep a strict inventory." He started to open the door.

"Sir, you said you thought Rick Teater was a great guy. Do you know anyone who doesn't feel that way?"

"Oh, there's some who didn't like him. Rick and I are business partners on this club, like I already told you. But some men got shafted in business dealings, especially in the early pool and spa days. I don't know any names to give you, and they'd have done something before now if they'd a mind to."

I touched his wrist. "I have one more question. If you hear anybody wanted to hurt Rick Teater or threatened him, will you call me?" I handed Ned one of my cards. "Sure thing."

"Thank you, Mr. Parks. Oh, by the way, what's that old house back there on the golf course? It seems out of place," I remarked, pointing in the direction of the shack.

"That old place was on my property when we built the club and course. Actually owned by a relative of mine—the property, I mean—and I bought it. That shack should be torn down, but I just haven't gotten around to it. I'm letting one of my maintenance boys live in it right now," Ned explained.

"So it's your property and Teater's money? Sounds like a good partnership."

"Oh, now don't get the wrong idea, Agent Hunter. I had to come up with plenty of money myself. This was no silver platter, and the upkeep'll be tremendous without his money backing it. As you'll find out, part of our agreement was if one of us died, the other became sole owner of the club. But that doesn't mean his money comes with it, just all the responsibility."

"I understand."

I left the Pro Shop and wandered around the parking lot, trying to come up with a way to get near the old building, at least two hundred yards away, without being seen by the maintenance crew. The practice range was full of golfers, and so were most of the fairways. I resigned myself to check it out later under the cover of darkness when I was less likely to get smacked by a shank.

9

Pepper Ellis got out of her Fiat wearing black trousers, a gold and black print top, and matching mules. She wasn't happy to see me, her eyes still red and swollen.

"Go away. Can't I grieve without your constant aggravation?" she hissed, starting up the stairs to the main entrance of her condominium.

"I'm sorry to bother you again, Ms. Ellis, but I need your help. I know it's tough. I'm not trying to be mean." I could see the wrenching pain in her face. Not the behavior of a murderer. I was nearly convinced she didn't kill Rick but maybe someone was trying to set her up. Nevertheless, I turned to walk back toward my car.

I heard a deep sigh. "Wait," she called. "Come on in."

I started up the steps before she changed her mind. The living room looked the same except for many music CD cases strewn around and several CDs on the couch and on top of the stereo. The chef went directly to the kitchen, buried her face in her hands, and leaned over on the kitchen island, saying nothing. I looked awkwardly around the room, really noticing it for the first time.

Her kitchen was glorious, the windows long with sheer white shades, scalloped at the bottom. The valances were made of scalloped print, cabbage roses on a bright gold background. The walls were green, and the floor, varnished oak. A nice mixture of old and modern. My eyes went to the sink: old porcelain on wooden legs. One stove was an old split-pea-colored porcelain and stainless steel gas model. The ultra-modern refrigerator had a clear glass front and a freezer drawer on the bottom. She leaned on a reconditioned antique table.

Above the island a long light reminded me of the ones over tavern pool tables with great lighting for cooking. Her round oak table and chairs fit in well. I could see her large pot collection hanging from an anchored wall rack near a glass cook top and Jenn-Air indoor grill. The chef lifted her head, looking straight at me.

"Rick will have to be buried as soon as his body's released. He has no family that I'm aware of. I have to bury him. Do you know how incredibly difficult this is? I'm trying to find some of his favorite music to play at the funeral." She drifted over to the sink and splashed cold water in her face. "If you don't think I killed him, why do you keep coming back here?" Her Carolina blue eyes turned and bored into mine.

"Ms. Ellis, I honestly don't think you killed him. I'm on to some other suspects, but I need your help to eliminate you completely."

"Okay. What do you need this time?"

"A recipe."

"You came here for a frickin' recipe? Geez, you're unbelievable!"

"Listen to me, Miss Ellis. The lab found stains on Rick's bed. Some kind of alcohol-based drink, probably tequila. Remember I told you about it? Anyway, the lab needs to know all the ingredients that would be in this drink so they can determine if anything else was added after you made them. Somebody obviously got one out of the fridge—either Mr. Teater or someone else." The woman gave me her undivided attention.

"Like maybe Chyna?"

"I can't say for sure."

"Oh, yeah. Well, I made some Margarita cheesecake freezes that morning and stuck them in Rick's fridge to have with our steaks. They aren't really drinks. They're desserts, but they do have tequila and triple sec in them, and I make them in goblets. I guess they're still there. I can tell you exactly what I put in them, if that'll help."

"It would help a lot." I pulled out my PDA and recorded as she listed off the ingredients.

"Cream cheese, powdered sugar, lime zest, lime juice, tequila, triple sec, some whipped cream, some regular granulated sugar, graham cracker crumbs, butter, and a little sea salt to rim the goblets. That's it. I made enough for four large servings. I left them in the fridge to firm up. I planned to salt the goblets before serving them, so they didn't have the salt. It's one of Rick's favorites," she said sadly.

"Thanks, I'll get this to the lab. Once again, I'm sorry to bother you. I'll let myself out."

I called the ingredients in to the lab in Raleigh, hoping it wouldn't take long to get a response. I told Charlie three more goblets should be in Teater's refrigerator for comparison, and that Ned Parks would call about his inventory before the day ended.

As I got ready to leave, I gave the police chief, wearing white slacks with a wrinkled denim shirt, its tail hanging out, the once-over. "By the way, what happened to Prince Charming?"

Charlie grinned. "He turned back into a frog." He warned me to be careful since a murderer lurked nearby.

"Logan, want to go out for a drink with me?" *Where did that come from?*

"Sorry, Charlie. I'm bummed. I'm heading for home. See you later." He'd taken my more than generous compliment far too seriously.

I went for a run and then flopped across the bed. I guess I dozed off because the phone startled me. I grabbed it and heard Ned Parks. He said he did have a rake missing and he was going to question every member of the club if he had to. I told Ned that Charlie and I would like to be there.

"Fine. Be here first thing in the morning. We open at eight. I'm starting then."

"Mr. Parks, can I make another request?"

"What?"

"I know this is your call, but could we keep the reason for doing this quiet? If one of your staff is a suspect, we don't want to scare him off."

He agreed to follow my instructions. I told him we'd be early.

I hung up the phone and pulled myself upright. It was getting dark; time to hit the nightspots again. Maybe I'd get lucky this time. At least I had identified Chyna. I showered, pulled on a blouse with a lace inset that showed a little tanned skin, and snatched my new turquoise capris off the closet rod. I went to the closet and hunted for my beaded slides.

After applying a bit too much makeup and some drop earrings, I surveyed myself in the full-length mirror. *Maybe I don't look too much like an agent.* I would start with Tramps, where I'd last seen Chyna Neary, hoping I wouldn't run into the police chief.

10

I got to the bar early and made my way to a booth in the corner so I could check out everyone already there, as well as any new arrivals. After about forty-five minutes I'd inhaled enough lung-burning smoke, and decided I might as well go, Chyna nowhere in the joint. I reached the door and gasped for clean, smoke-free air.

I drove up the beach to Skeeter's, a classier bar, often frequented by the more affluent crowd. I tucked my revolver into my purse with my pepper spray and stun gun since I had no room in my capris. As I pulled up, I saw Chyna going in the door alone. It would be helpful if she stayed that way.

I parked and went inside. Chyna sat at the bar on an upholstered stool. I looked around for a booth, and not finding an empty one, I headed for a stool. I nodded at Chyna.

"Logan! Good to see you again," said the barkeep, one of my high school friends.

"Hey, Clint! Good to see you too," I said, hoping he wouldn't say anything about my being an agent in front of a possible suspect. The place was hopping, so he stayed busy filling drink orders. I ordered a virgin Strawberry

Margarita. Chyna ordered a frozen drink too. I surveyed her in the bar mirror as often as I thought I could without drawing suspicion. My attention momentarily fell on a huge man at a table behind her, who spilled over both sides of a plastic chair. I could envision the chair bending and sinking, eventually giving way, and dumping him on the cement floor. I was thirsty so I turned around to nurse the drink Clint sat in front of me.

"Yum! Good drink," I said, winking at Clint, who smiled as he headed to the other end of the long bar.

Chyna looked up, and her eyes seemed to cut through me. "Oh, these ain't too good. I had one that was awesome. It had cream cheese in it, real thick. Yum." She ran her tongue around her inferno red lips. I couldn't tell if she was stoned, or just had on a pound of eyeliner and mascara. Her raven hair was tangled, and two long strands fell down across her nose. Gorgeous, just made up to look trashy.

Chyna wore a several-cup-sizes-too-small black bustier with a sheer blouse over it, advertising two of her best assets. She'd poured herself into gold tights with a purple organdy sash tied around her tiny waist, and gold stilettos adorned with beads. *Excessively flashy, but great attention-getters.*

"Who would put cream cheese in a margarita?"

Clint, now back on this end of the bar, had been half-listening. "Not us. Only the chefs get that fancy," he said, going back to the other end of the bar. "Sounds like a dessert drink to me."

"What's a good drink here?" I asked her with a smile. Chyna slid over a stool and whispered, "They ain't got none," she laughed loud, too close to my ear for comfort. "You have to go to a fancy place, like Clint said, to get a really good drink. This is about as good as you'll find around here, though." Chyna fell silent and went back to sipping her drink. I finished mine, trying to decide what to do next. I didn't intend to get drunk, and I didn't want to leave. I had to find a way to get her alone to ask her some questions. I didn't want to show my badge or manhandle her in front of the bar crowd.

The music got louder. Several men came over and whispered in her ear, but she shrugged them off. She seemed to be moody, laughing one minute, looking miserable the next. Finally she got up, threw some bills on the bar, and walked out the door alone. I paid my tab and tried not to follow too closely behind her. As I reached the door, I saw her walking toward the parking lot entrance with her head hung low. I called out to her, "Hey, miss, you need a lift?"

Chyna turned and gave me the once over. "No! Leave me the hell alone."

I watched where she went, toward the south near the edge of the road. I ambled toward my car, still trying to keep her in sight. She sauntered slowly, and I got into my car and pulled around the lot enough to continue watching her.

I inched the Beemer out into the road, glad no traffic came between us. Suddenly I saw something in the road and stepped out to reach for the organdy sash she'd dropped.

She walked on for about a mile and ducked under some low trees and onto a dirt path. I turned my lights off. Once she disappeared, I pulled my Beemer over and waited a few minutes. She didn't reappear. I pulled out my revolver, grabbed the sash, and locked my purse in the car.

I crept under the trees, making out a small weather-beaten wood-framed house I never knew existed. The paint was peeling, and some storm shutters dangled by one nail head. I worked my way up to the porch and tried to look in a window, but the shades were pulled and the tears in them were too high up for me to peek through. I eased back toward the door, took a deep breath, and knocked.

Chyna opened the door and stabbed me once again with her eyes. "You! Did you follow me, you bitch?"

I held out the sash. "You dropped this. I wanted to give it back." I looked around her into the room. She snatched the sash from my hands, and saw my gun.

She screamed and backed into the room. "Don't kill me! What do you want?" It hadn't been my intention to get into the house this way, but here I was, and so far, it was working. I pulled out my SBI badge and showed it to her.

"My name is Logan Hunter. I'm not here to hurt you." A nervous Chyna fumbled back onto a worn dung brown loveseat. She began to twist the sash in her hands, almost to the point of wringing the beads off.

"Do you live here alone?"

"Y…Yeah. Look, I don't want no trouble. Whata ya want?" Chyna's eyes bulged as though looking around for a way out or a heavy object and an opportunity to use it. I made myself as comfortable as possible on a ragged hassock between her and the door.

"I'm investigating the death of Rick Teater. I understand you knew him."

Chyna shook her head, more hair falling into her eyes. "No, No, you're mistaken. I don't know nobody by that name." Chyna's face had become colorless even with the excessive makeup.

"No?" I gave her a second to change her answer. "Look, Chyna, I'm going to be straight up with you. You were seen with Rick Teater the night he died. I have a witness." Chyna sat motionless, not making a sound.

"I could take you to the police station to interrogate you. I'm trying to do you a favor here. I've got some questions, and I need your cooperation."

Chyna jumped up and ran for the door. I dove off the hassock and managed to grab her stiletto and trip her. She fell face first on the floor, scrambled up, and tried to get away from me, but I rushed her and kept her from getting out the door. I knew if she got outside, I'd have a devil of a time finding her in the dark in her familiar surroundings. Chyna squealed and twitched like a rabbit caught in eagle talons.

"Okay, have it your way." I slapped the police-issued cuffs on her tiny wrists. She kicked, groaned, and spat but didn't yell. Wrestling her to the Beemer was an exhausting exercise.

11

I got Chyna into the front seat and checked her feet—
every toe in its entirety.

A shocked police chief answered my call, and said he
would meet me at the station. All the way I prayed I hadn't
committed a major blunder. This isn't the way I'd planned
the evening. *Hell, I really hadn't planned at all. I should have just
badged my way in.*

Charlie was there when I arrived with Chyna. I parked
at the door so we could usher her in with as little commotion
as possible. We didn't want everyone on the beach to know
I'd hauled her in.

Charlie offered Chyna some coffee and she spat like a
wild cat, cursing vividly. She writhed and twitched every
way possible, but the handcuffs held. We decided to let her
wear herself out before trying to question her.

"Look, I've known Chyna for years. Give me a few
minutes alone with her, and I'm sure she'll cooperate,"
Charlie whispered. I nodded and stepped out, taking my
time to collect an out-of-date tape recorder and two tapes
from Maggie's desk. I walked back into the room. Chyna
said something about a ring.

I glanced at Charlie. "She says she's seen a ring that might have belonged to Mr. Teater," he stated while Chyna kept her eyes riveted on him. We sat quietly for a few minutes, waiting for our guest to talk. I finally motioned Charlie out of the room with me.

"Look, she's not talking. She's staring at you like she hates your guts."

Charlie grimaced and laughed weakly. "That's because I've brought her in a hundred times, starting about age fourteen. I ain't her favorite person, that's for sure."

"Let me talk to her alone for a minute, Charlie."

"No way! This is my station, my jurisdiction!"

"I'm not trying to take over, but we're not getting anywhere, and if we turn her loose…"

We argued for a few minutes, and he reluctantly agreed. He stuck his head in and told Chyna he would be right outside the door, so she'd better do what she knew she was supposed to do. I went inside and closed the door.

"You don't like us much, huh?"

"I don't like you a lot, but you're better than banana nose, I reckon."

"Chyna, what's the deal with you and Charlie?" She squirmed around and glanced toward the door.

"You can speak freely. He's gone to his car to get some things."

"He's a dirty old man is all. He's always gropin' me and sayin' nasty stuff when nobody else is around."

"Charlie? Really? But, don't you think that goes with your occupation?"

Her head drooped and she shrugged. "Please. I've gotta get out of here. He's gonna kill me."

I walked over to her. "Who's going to kill you?" I rested my butt cheek on the table beside her. Chyna looked at me, her eyes now sad and scared, mascara running down her face. Charlie eased back in, nodding at Chyna, as I pressed *Record*.

"I ain't got nothin' to do with it, I swear. Please let me go. He'll kill me if he finds out I'm here."

Charlie pulled up a chair and sat near her, opening a piece of paper. "Chyna, you need to cooperate with us. This here's a murder investigation. If you know anything, you have to tell us. Every detail. This fax I just got from the lab says your fingerprints are all over Teater's back door and a wine glass. I'd say you're up to your pretty little ass in murder. And, of course, we can always charge you with prostitution."

I moved closer. I offered her a tissue, and she patted her thick, glittery eyelids. "Chyna, you told me earlier about a margarita made with cream cheese. Where've you had one of those?"

She tried to get the cuffs off, becoming more agitated in the process. "You can't keep me here. I ain't done nothin' wrong!"

"Chyna, we have a witness who saw you in bed with Rick Teater the night he died. Now we have your prints to prove you were there. I suggest you cooperate with us," I told her, leaning in. Her face blanched.

"We can go ahead and book you for prostitution and homicide. At least the night won't have been a waste," Charlie added, reaching for official forms.

"You need to call an attorney," I suggested as I turned the recorder off.

Chyna gave a long sigh and lifted her eyes to meet mine. Tears began to flow. I told her I'd take the cuffs off if she'd cooperate. We promised her temporary protection. Chyna nodded. We offered her time to call an attorney but she declined, signing a release that stated her willingness to talk in exchange for protection.

"If you try to run, I'm going to lock your ass up and we're leaving for the night. Then you're on your own with no protection," Charlie said, making sure he made good eye contact. "Comprende'?"

He uncuffed her and motioned to another wood table and chair. He left to arrange protective custody. I let her stew a few minutes, waiting for Charlie. Then we positioned ourselves so we were between the door and our guest.

"Let's get one thing straight. If I tell you what I know, you have to get me outta this town. Hide me. I swear to you he'll come lookin' for me."

I nodded and mashed *Record* once again.

Chyna began. "Linc and I hang out together a lot when we're not workin'."

Charlie raised his arm to stop her. "You need to be specific about names, places, and events."

Chyna sighed deeply. "His name is Lincoln, but everybody calls him Linc. He works at Genesis Golf and Country Club. I've known him since he moved here to do yard maintenance."

"What's his last name?" I inquired.

"Tumu. He's part Hawaiian or somethin'. I met him at Tramps. Linc moved here to get away from his old man in Atlantic City. Mr. Parks hired him at the golf course. Linc and his dad didn't get along. He talks about his old man all the time. That's all I know."

"Please describe Lincoln Tumu, and tell us the story from start to finish. We'll try not to interrupt," Charlie said.

"Linc ain't much bigger than I am. His hair's dark as mine, and he wears it kinda long for a guy. He wants to be a surfer, but we ain't got no waves big enough to ride here, and he don't look too good no way. Well, I see him around a lot, and one night after we left Tramps he wanted me to go with him for a walk down the beach. We skinny-dipped and walked down the beach for a while real late at night.

"We came to a place on the beach where Linc kissed me and turned me around to see the mansion on the hill.

I'd seen it plenty of times, but I'd never been near it. The sign said 'Private Property'. Anyway, Linc said the man who lived there owed him a lot of money and refused to pay him. Pissed him off big time. He cussed and raised hell about this Mr. Teater screwin' him over. He said Mr. Teater threatened him and had enough money to have him fired or run off the beach.

Chyna guzzled the drink Charlie set in front of her, cleared her throat, and continued. "Linc said he wanted me to help him with a plan. I told him 'No' but then he gave me a sleeve, and I told him I would."

"A sleeve?" I asked.

"A hundred dollar bill," Charlie said to me.

"We went back to his house near Genesis, where the pro is lettin' him stay rent-free. He got out some beers and pot and started tellin' me his plan. He wanted me to flirt with Mr. Teater and get into the mansion. I was supposed to drug him with some stuff Linc would give me. I asked him if the drug would kill him and he said 'No, it'll just make him real groggy.' Linc wanted me to leave a door open so he could get in and go through Teater's wallet while we were in bed." Chyna hung her head again.

I coaxed, "But that's not what happened."

Chyna shook her head. "No, that asshole Linc had some stuff to put in Mr. Teater's drink at Skeeter's. He found out Mr. Teater and some other guys had played golf, and the guys he played with wanted to have a drink together. Linc found out where they were goin' by eavesdroppin' and then picked me up. I flirted with the bartender long enough for Linc to put some white stuff in Mr. Teater's drink. I don't have no idea what it was—some kind of pills crushed up, I think. Linc winked at me and went to a dark booth to watch Mr. Teater from across the room.

"After a while the golfers got up to leave, and I left the bar stool and walked out behind Mr. Teater. I dropped my purse deliberately and everything spilled out near him. He turned and smiled at me, and I bent over to pick up my lipstick that rolled over close to his foot. I had on a tight tube top. He was watchin' me more than pickin' up things, that's for sure."

"Linc watched from inside the bar. Mr. Teater handed me my pen, mascara, and a tube of lipstick, and I held onto his hand long enough to show him I was interested. He had a beautiful smile, but he turned my hand loose. He went to his convertible and drove off. I told Linc he didn't seem to be drugged. Linc said it would take effect once he got home."

Chyna shifted and coughed. "Look, I've told you too much already. Linc won't let this slide, I'm tellin' you!" She grew louder and more agitated.

"Chyna, a man is dead. If you can help us find the killer, you have to do that. Don't you have a conscience? Besides, we've already told you several times we have a plan in place to protect you if you're in danger," Charlie emphasized from close range.

Chyna continued. "I swear, I didn't even know the man was dead until I heard it on TV. Then I knew. I never saw Mr. Teater again after I left that night, and he was alive then." She stood up and leaned toward me. "I swear to you, he was alive."

12

Chyna poured the rest her soft drink into the coffee she'd let get cold. We stayed close by waiting for her to begin again.

"Tell us what happened next," I said, running low on patience.

"Linc and I started down the beach toward the mansion. He took some kind of rake to wipe out our tracks. Fifteen minutes later we got to the steps that go up the hill. Linc took off his sandals and socks and stuck'em under the bottom step in case he needed to run fast. I didn't want to go, but Linc insisted that everything would be all right, and so we started the second part of Linc's plan. It was gettin' dark, so we went around the gazebo to see if Mr. Teater wasn't out at the pool. Linc hid in some flowery bushes near the gazebo while I went around to the back door and rang the bell.

"I was expectin' the maid, you know, Kiko, but Mr. Teater came to the door himself, wearin' bathin' trunks." I made a note that Chyna called the maid Kiko as if she were familiar with her. "He was wobbly, kind of staggerin', like the stuff was takin' effect. He smiled at me and opened the

door. I told him I was sorry to bother him, but I was missin'
a few items from my purse, and did he have them.

"He asked me to come in, lookin' a little confused. He
had what looked like a thick margarita in his hand. He set it
down, stuck the spoon in it, and mumbled somethin' about
checkin' his golf shorts pockets. He headed for the stairs
and went up. I sipped the drink thing. It was real good, and
I could taste cream cheese and tequila. I put some more of
the stuff Linc gave me in it. I figured as thick as it was, he
wouldn't know the difference. I made sure the door was
unlocked for Linc, took the margarita, and went upstairs.
By that time Linc could see me from outside.

"I found Mr. Teater sittin' on the side of his bed going
through his pants pockets, still mutterin' somethin' I couldn't
understand. I heard him say somethin' about pepper. I
walked over to the bed, and he looked up, kind of holdin'
his head. I asked him if he felt all right and handed him his
drink, sayin' it might make him feel better. It had got soupier
by then.

"He drank most of it, and put the glass down on the
nightstand. By this time, I was close to him, so he couldn't
get off the bed without movin' me. I put my hands on his
shoulders and pushed him backwards. He fell right over.
He never even reached for me. I swear I didn't kill him. He
was alive!" Chyna banged her fist on the table.

"Okay," I started, excited about all the details. "Where
was Linc all this time?"

"I don't know. By the time I pushed Mr. Teater over on
the bed I thought I heard him, but he never came in the
room. I straddled Mr. Teater and took off my shorts and
top. I figured I could at least turn him a good trick since we
were robbin' him."

"So, did you?"

Chyna shook her head. "The man was too far gone to
have any fun. I don't think he knew where the hell he was.

Probably didn't even know he was in his own house. He passed out on the bed, still alive. I swear to you! I started hearin' a loud noise, like pots and pans bangin' around, so I grabbed my clothes, and ran out the back door. I never looked back.

"When I got down to the beach, I told Linc somebody was in the house. He said he saw the chef come in, but couldn't warn me. He told me to take off, and he started rakin' my tracks. I asked him if he got the wallet, and he said 'No', but he'd go back later since Mr. Teater would be out a long time. He wanted to wait until the coast was clear, eight or after. He grabbed my throat and said if I told anybody about any of it, he'd kill me. And he meant it too! I ran.

"I swear to you I never saw Linc again until a couple of nights ago. He threatened me and roughed me up a little. But that ain't nothin' new," concluded Chyna, looking at Charlie.

"Why did he rough you up?" I had to ask.

"Linc came over to my place and barged in. We did some gas and he started shootin' his mouth off. I asked him where he got the money for drugs, and he said he pawned a Rolex and some other stuff and had plenty of money. I told him I knew Mr. Teater was dead, and he said he didn't do it, and I said 'You told me you wouldn't kill him, Linc' and he grabbed me, threw me down, and said to keep my mouth shut or I'd regret it."

"So," Charlie figured, "Linc went back. If there was a tussle, he killed Teater. But if Teater was as drugged as you say, how in the hell did he get into the hot tub?"

Chyna shrugged. "Look, I ain't never said Linc killed Mr. Teater. I don't know what happened." We nodded.

I made a note to contact forensics and have a look at the entire autopsy report. *Were there any marks on Rick's heels to indicate he'd been dragged from upstairs to the hot tub? Had they ever determined what drugs were in his body? Could drugs have been the cause of death?*

"Chyna, you knew the maid's name. How do you know her?"

She fumbled around, glanced at Charlie, and finally answered. "Umm, she hangs out at some of the same places I do is all. I just know her first name. I don't know nothin' else about her."

"You told us what you were wearing at Teater's. For the record, what was Linc wearing?"

She thought for a second. "Basically the same cheesy stuff he always wears—slouchy khaki shorts, a raggedy shirt, brown sandals, and socks. He always has to wear those stupid tube socks even in the summer time."

"Why?"

"He has a deformed toe. He never really told me nothin' about what happened, but part of it's missin'," Chyna explained.

I gave Charlie a nod attached to a gigantic smile.

"I don't know nothin' else. What can I do now? Linc'll be lookin' for me as soon as you let me go."

Charlie went to the exterior door to answer a soft knock. Marcia Grady, a mainland deputy and old classmate of mine, came in and nodded in my direction. Charlie told Chyna he would try to help her since she'd cooperated. Chyna hesitated, muttering something about not having any choice. She glanced back at me with despondent eyes, hung her head, and disappeared through the door with Marcia.

I looked Charlie over, his salt-and-pepper hair a mess from rubbing his hands through it so much, his blue shirttail half out again, his pants full of wrinkles, and that bulbous nose almost purple. I decided if I looked as bad as he did, we both needed a few hours of sleep before tackling Lincoln Tumu. I supposed the way I'd handled Chyna had added to his stress.

Charlie assigned Max stake out at Tumu's house to make sure he didn't run. If we were lucky, he didn't know I'd brought Chyna in. And that, in itself, had been lucky. My plan had been only to talk to her, but she'd created the scene that led to the late night interrogation.

It never hurts to have luck on your side.

I admit I was relieved to take Pepper Ellis off the suspect list. I wanted to let her know that not only was she off the hook, but Rick Teater wasn't having sex with a hooker. He'd been faithful to her. He was simply too incapacitated to take care of himself.

I phoned the lab and the results from the goblet were in. Significant traces of Valium were found in it along with plenty of tequila and triple sec, indicating that Chyna told us the truth.

"Mixing enough Valium with alcohol *could* have been lethal, but I don't think that's what killed him," Howie explained. "Logan, the autopsy revealed severe internal bruising of the head, neck and chest, but I can't account for why there are no bruises on the outside of his body. Except for his heels. Teater was beaten to death with some sort of blunt object, not yet identified." He said he had enough evidence to release the body for burial, and he'd contact Mr. Rhodes, Teater's attorney.

"Howie, did you say Teater had bruises on his feet?"

"Yeah, as a matter of fact, the backs of both heels were bruised."

"Could that have happened by being dragged down the stairs?"

"Sure could."

I filled Charlie in on the lab report and told him I'd meet him at Genesis Beach Golf Club at eight in the morning, only a few hours away. We had plenty of questions for Linc Tumu.

Pepper stayed on my mind. This had been a horrible ordeal for her, and it wasn't over yet. It was now time to bury Rick Teater.

13

The nightmare had me tossing and thrashing all night, pulling all the bedding loose. I'd been up enough to mess up the house, and the blinds on the surfside were askew. I'd been sleepwalking again. I'd learned to lock myself in, since I had this thing about trying to get out through a window. I still couldn't remember any details of the nightmare, other than the bony hand with long fingers leaving me feeling uneasy, like something ominous approached.

The morning was much cooler and breezier than I expected, but the sun would warm the chill off quickly. I headed for my appointment with Ned Parks at Genesis Golf Club. I arrived early, but a few cars were already there. Ned came out to greet me, and we went straight to his office and closed the door.

I told him I was certain one of his employees had taken the rake, and I wanted to question that employee, namely Linc Tumu, and if necessary, he would be escorted to the police station for interrogation, but I wanted to question him in a non-threatening environment first.

Ned agreed to cooperate. He said Linc was a temperamental young man, some days friendly, other days

distant, but he'd never known Linc to be disrespectful. Rick
Teater liked him enough to request him as his caddy, and
had tried to help him with college tuition until Rick figured
out he used the money for drugs and hadn't registered for
college at all. Perhaps Rick had been too trusting of Lincoln
Tumu.

Ned answered a rap on the door. Charlie winked at me
and shook hands with Ned.

"Charlie, you've got yourself a fine helper here."

"Yep, Logan is a sharp cookie."

They engaged in small talk for a few minutes while I
looked out onto the beach from the pro's back window. I
could see several young men walking from both directions,
headed for the Pro Shop to caddy on this cool morning.

I looked back out into the front parking lot and saw a
Jeep pull in. I recognized Linc, with his dark brown shoulder-
length hair, a strand dangling in his left eye. *At least he and
Chyna have hairstyles in common.* The caddies talked and laughed
as they approached the Pro Shop, but Linc seemed a little
removed from them, heading toward the cart shed. Ned
called out to them to come inside. "You too, Tumu."

All the caddies and Linc entered, Ned addressing each
one of them. Charlie and I stayed in Ned's office with the
door slightly ajar so I could see Linc clearly. He had
diminutive eyes and almost no lips. His nose seemed a little
too prominent for his other features. He held his mouth
tightly shut, as if he tense. He couldn't see me, and didn't
appear to suspect anything. I noted that he wore tube socks.

Club members came in the doors and selected their usual
caddy, or waited to be assigned one. The clubhouse cleared
quickly, and Linc was assigned to Alice Garris, one of the
few older ladies. Ned figured Alice would be slow getting
out of the clubhouse, and we could corner Linc before he
got out on the fairways with her.

Linc left the clubhouse, got into a cart, and went to the parking lot to get Alice's clubs while she headed for the restroom.

Charlie stood near the main door, and, when Linc walked back in, I approached him from across the room. Ned stayed to the side. "Lincoln Tumu?" I asked with my most professional voice and demeanor.

Linc stopped in his tracks. "Yeah…whata ya want?" He glared. I approached and presented my badge. He started backing up toward the door and Charlie moved around behind him.

"Linc, they have a few questions for all the Genesis staff—about Rick Teater. No need to spook," Ned insisted. "They're going to talk to everyone. You're just the first of many."

I could tell Linc wasn't buying it. I motioned him to a wood bench near a putter display. "I need for you to remove your socks and shoes," I demanded, realizing instantly I'd moved too hastily.

"No!" Linc shot back at me. "I ain't done nothin,' and I ain't gonna be treated no criminal. You got somethin' on me, take me in. You got a warrant to search me?" Linc was in my face too close for comfort, his tight mouth now an angry sneer. Charlie was right behind him to make sure I didn't get punched.

Ned came closer. "Just cooperate, Linc. It won't take but a minute and you and Alice can take off." Linc realized the doorway was now open, so he bolted, none of us quick enough to catch him, in his Jeep and gone in a matter of seconds.

"Damn it!" I yelled, throwing my pen down the front steps. Charlie patched through to several mainland deputies to move fast so Linc couldn't get off the island, and if he did, to have roadblocks set up on the mainland.

"He got away because of me. I'd moved in too fast, just like a damn rookie." I kicked my shoes on the pavement.

"Not to worry, Logan. He won't get far. He just incriminated himself. Regardless of which way he goes, he'll be got," Charlie said with great confidence. I, on the other hand, wasn't so confident. Not that I didn't think local law enforcement was good at what they did, but there weren't many of us, and Linc was extremely familiar with the beach.

We ran to our vehicles, yelling the different directions we would go. I turned into every beach path, looking for Jeep tracks, while Charlie and I radioed back and forth and with the others in pursuit. Max joined the hunt, but after several hours, we were getting nowhere.

Lincoln Tumu had disappeared. If the only road off the beach was blocked, he had to be here somewhere unless he got across before the roadblock.

We decided to meet and draw up a plan of action so we weren't overlapping each other. We left two deputies to continue the roadblock, checking every vehicle carefully before it left the beach. Two other deputies and Max and I all met at Hot Dog Haven, and Charlie laid out a map of the beach on the round white table beside the stand. I ordered two-dozen slaw dogs all the way and five Pepsis. We chowed down and grabbed our directives. Time to haul ass.

I went out on my own. I checked my revolver. Loaded. I checked my heart. Pounding in my throat. I had strict orders to call in if I found anything or needed backup.

I couldn't drive up close to Linc's place, so I had to leave my Beemer about one hundred yards away on a street. As I parked, the weather came on my radio:

"A tropical depression that started in the gulf has swept across the Florida panhandle, weakened, and come back out in the Gulf Stream. It's now expected to return to tropical storm intensity as it approaches the North Carolina coastline, bringing with it torrential downpours and high winds as early as this afternoon. We are now under a tornado watch."

Great. A suspected murderer on the loose, and a tropical storm almost on top of us. I could already see dark clouds beginning to circle the sky like a wagon train. I prayed Tumu hadn't made it off the beach to the mainland. I didn't see a Jeep, but that didn't mean Linc wasn't there. He could've abandoned it and walked up the beach. I could have a riflescope trained on me at this moment. I gulped a few times, prayed, and moved toward the old house with my gun drawn.

I managed to get around some big clumps of sea grass and follow a path to the old white board house. I tiptoed across the rickety porch to the door as quietly as I could. Not locked. I eased it open. *What a mess.* I didn't have to look far to find many pairs of tube socks with various colors of stripes. I checked the small house, pointing my gun around every corner as I got to each room. No sign of Linc. As much as I wanted to search for evidence, finding Linc was more urgent. My radio started beeping *Low Battery.*

I swung by the station to get a fresh battery pack. Maggie, alone with all phone lines ringing and the radios squawking at the same time, was vitally important in receiving and dispatching information to all officers and troopers who called in. Charlie had always trusted her with information, and the excitement had her in a frenzied state. She appeared to have at least six hands as she handed me a note while dispatching information to one of the officers. She affirmed the tropical storm had moved back over the warm ocean water, predicted to make a sharp turn north, right on top of us.

Charlie set up a network from the ocean to the highway, which, in most places, was only about one mile. If Linc didn't show up, a house-to-house search would begin. I radioed Charlie to see if he wanted me to call the Coast Guard for a helicopter. I'd already been through the marina, checking to see if any small boats were missing. It wasn't that far across the sound to freedom.

"Great idea. Do it if you think we can catch him before this storm breaks."

The copter arrived forty-five minutes later. I'd never ridden in one, but the pilot didn't know what Tumu looked like, so I took a deep breath, hopped in, and buckled up. We headed over the water and down the beach. The helicopter lights illuminated the dramatic, frantically moving ocean with its large rough swells. A strong breeze erupted into stronger wind gusts, so the pilot was on alert for sudden turbulence. Palm trees shuddered and bent as we hurried by. We turned up the beach, combing it from the ocean to the sound. Cars, trucks and RVs were lined up, sitting still on the one road to the mainland.

A strong gust of wind prompted the pilot to grip the controls while I gripped my bladder. I called Charlie to see what was going on. He said some folks were leaving even though an evacuation order hadn't been issued. Many locals had learned the hard way that this island was too thin to withstand even minor storm winds and the accompanying surges. Nor'easters sometimes ran them to the mainland. Charlie squawked that the troopers were checking every vehicle thoroughly to make sure Linc wasn't evacuating with someone.

The wind blasted repeatedly and the pilot said he couldn't stay up much longer. He still had to fly back to base camp twenty miles away. The first storm bands had arrived and brought darkness.

Someone was talking on the radio, but the chopper was too loud to hear. As we made a turn to start back toward the ocean, I saw a flash of light and something glanced off the helicopter's metal base. I could hear now; Charlie yelled, "Get away! Get away!"

"We're being shot at!"

"Damn!" yelled the pilot. "Nobody told me I'd be a friggin' target. Let's get the hell outta here." In a split second we were over the ocean too far away for another shot. I put the radio to my ear and heard Charlie order, "Move in."

Well, well. Lincoln Tumu is a dumb ass; his shot showed the police his exact location.

The pilot circled around to where we could see blue lights and activity. He put his searchlight on the ground and into some beach brush. Several law enforcement officers, with drawn guns, moved in toward thick twisted sea brush thrashing violently. I motioned to the pilot to take me back to the station. I wanted to be sitting there when they brought Linc in. I thanked the pilot, who radioed that he was returning to base camp and away from the storm. I wished him a safe trip and hopped out.

14

Maggie and I waited for an update. I paced the floor while she finished off a Whopper.

"Want tha poke froies?" she asked, shoving the fry bag toward me. I reached for them.

"Thanks."

She touched my wrist. "Logan, have you noticed any change in Charlie?"

"What do you mean?"

"He's acting like a wampus cat. That man actually came in heah yesterdy and snuggled up to me and rubbed my back until Oi got up and moved away from 'im. Oi can't be sure, but Oi think he humped the chair behind me. He's never been this way. Somethin's not roight. He's actin' squirrelly. Oi'm knockin' the hell out of 'im if he does it again, job or no job."

"I hadn't noticed. I'll try to pay more attention to him. You might want to reconsider assaulting a law-enforcement officer though."

"Well, Oi've worked close to that man for yeahs and he's never been auit o' the way, you know?"

"Maybe he's just got the hots for you, Maggie, or it could be male menopause." I smiled and glanced at my watch.

"Damn it, they should have been here by now!"

A car screeched to a stop near the door. The station door slammed open and a disheveled Max stepped into the room. He looked at us and shook his head. "We can't zero in on him. He's a slippery bastard," Max said, noticeably disappointed.

I jumped up into Max's face. "Whata ya mean? I thought you had him!"

He turned red and shook his head. "Turned out to be that crazy old coot, Joey Black who got messed up in 'Nam. He's off his medication. He thought the chopper was Viet Cong. No sign of Tumu," Max muttered, walking past me.

"Well, I'm outta here. Catch you later, Maggie," I said, heading out the door.

Max grabbed my arm. "Wait a second, Logan. Charlie and the deputies are searching where Chyna stayed. I guess we need to wait for orders."

I gave him a stern look. "Stay here and wait if you want to, Max, but we've got a murder suspect and a tropical storm. The wind is creating all kinds of shadows to trick us. The rain'll start any second. The longer we wait, the better chance Linc has of getting away. I'm going to the club and have a look around. Linc's familiar with that place. Maybe he'll head there while you're sitting on your ass." I'd never been good at taking orders anyway.

Max backed off. I reached for the door and the wind caught it, slamming it back against the wall and sending papers flying from Maggie's desk. I let out a whispered "Sorry" and disappeared into a gust of sand.

I ran to the Beemer and started it as Max snatched the passenger side door open and jumped in. I smiled and headed toward the country club, glad to have the company as increasing wind speed tossed the old car around. I drove up as close to the Pro Shop and outbuildings as I could.

Max and I left the car with flashlights and guns, and my short hair immediately flew into my eyes. I struggled to the Pro Shop and looked for any broken glass or jimmied locks while Max maneuvered around the outside of the building. The storm had erased all footprints. I prowled around the cart shed, checking every cart, looking in it, around it, and through it. Lincoln Tumu wasn't there.

I worked my way back to the Beemer at an erratic pace, sometimes being pushed from behind and often stopped in mid-stride. The sustained wind had strengthened and the sand unmercifully stung my legs, arms, and face.

Max appeared out of the windstorm, his pants leg blowing high enough I could see his red striped socks. My heart skipped.

Whoa! Max wears striped socks?

He hopped in.

"What?" he asked, huffing to catch his breath.

I must have stared. "Nothing."

We bullied the car doors closed and took a few deep breaths. I liked Max, but the socks worried me. We'd checked the golf club together, and I'd felt safe with him. But should I? Charlie and mainland deputies were doing house-to-house searches, which could take all night.

If Max and I stay together, I'm going to keep both eyes on him.

"Max, come in, Max." Charlie's voice boomed through the airwaves.

"Max, Chief."

"You with Logan? Get over here. I need you right now."

"Yes, sir, I'm with Logan. Have you got him?"

"No, but I need for you and Logan to split up. We don't have enough manpower to double up." I dropped Max off at the station to get his own car and spun back out into the storm.

If Linc wanted a safe place to hide, where would he go?

Wait a minute! It hit me. I tried to get through to Maggie, but my radio only squawked at me. I tried my cell phone. I'd forgotten to charge it. Anyway, I was going with my intuition. The hell with phones and radios. I couldn't afford to lose time getting fresh ones.

I parked my car in the Public Access area near the dunes at TideLand. I could already see waves lapping over the top of the dunes way down the beach. What I was about to do wasn't smart, the wind enough to knock me down, and a wave surge with undertows could easily pull me underwater. Tropical storms always brought rip currents, and high tide could be a bastard.

I decided to enter the estate by the beach, in case Linc was inside and looking for us to come to the front. I pulled up my trouser leg and wrapped the ankle pocket around it, inserting my .25 caliber pistol that even Charlie was unaware I had. I got to the yellow crime tape, now broken and flapping in the wind.

I crouched on the bottom step, already wet from a few lofty waves. I gathered my courage, said a prayer, drew my revolver, and started my ascent. The twisted trees slapped me around and scratched my skin. The hill had never seemed so steep. My lips stung with sand and salt, the texture like grits. The only protection my eyes had were the small wire-framed glasses that managed to stay wrapped around my ears.

Tropical wind almost knocked me off the path and into the sea grass and dunes. I pushed my way forward and finally reached the gazebo, where the whale weather vane spun furiously again. I wondered if it could survive this storm. I peeked around the gazebo and couldn't see anything but dark tree shadows everywhere, bowing and nodding.

The torrential rain began suddenly, and I caught my breath in the gazebo. I dug the radio—now officially dead—out of my pocket and crammed it back in, checked the gun in my hand again, and leaned around the edge of the gazebo. I would be out in the open once I left it until I reached the back entrance of the house, which seemed miles away. I had to make a run for it, past the long pool and through the domed arbor. My skin crawled. I really wished I had some back up, but nobody knew my location. I'd broken Rule Number One of Criminal Justice 101: Always notify headquarters of your location and don't go alone. But sometimes it couldn't be helped.

My adrenalin surged and I took off, running full speed around the pool area, slipping once I reached the cover of the arbor. My feet shot out from under me, and I landed hard on the wet light gold cement. I let out a yelp and managed to hang on to my gun.

I pulled myself up and darted behind a crepe myrtle bush to rub my bottom. Nothing seemed to be broken, but I knew I'd be sore. I slapped back at the bush that beat me relentlessly, ready to get inside, out of the storm. I got to the back door, at last out of the wind and stinging rain. I felt as though I'd been beaten half to death.

The bottom pane of door glass had been broken. My pulse went into overdrive. I turned the knob and opened the unlocked door, entering the room as quietly as the storm would allow. The house wasn't as neat and clean as it was on my prior visits. It was still a crime scene and should have been off limits for everyone.

I pulled out my pen light near the drained hot tub, sandy shoe prints leading me toward the hall and kitchen. I squelched the urge to flip the light switch and eased slowly around the room, gun pointed, my tiny light giving my location away. I shifted to the door of the main house, looked about again, and peeked out into the hallway. No sign of anyone. I moved out into the hall and down to the first door. I pushed the door open to reveal a half bath.

Back in the hall I opened the next door, behind it a library with many bookshelves lining the threshold and the exterior wall. A baby grand piano sat near the windows. I crouched to look under and around it. Nothing. Various pictures of Rick Teater and friends, including Pepper Ellis, and a large assortment of sailboats and hand-made pottery were on display.

I maneuvered back out into the hall and around to the huge kitchen. Food wrappers on the island and an empty soft drink bottle near the refrigerator betrayed the trespasser. I worked my way toward the laundry room with my gun ready. I nudged the door and whipped my light inside the small room. Unless Linc had curled up in the dryer, he wasn't there either.

I moved back to the hall and stopped at the stairwell, taking a deep breath.

He could be waiting for me to get to the top of the stairs.

I decided to crawl up in case he planned to throw me down them, it would be a harder task. I heard a noise and jumped. It sounded like a tree went down somewhere outside. The rain beat hard enough on the windows that I wondered how they could hold up. The storm had an adverse effect on my nerves and my ability to hear movement inside the house. I could feel my pulse throbbing around the butt of my gun. I doused my light.

I bent down and began to crawl with my .38 pointed up the stairs. I made it to the top and peered down the hall each way. Slowly I opened the door to a bedroom, masculine with a large heavy dark oak bed covered in heavy tapestry for a beach house. An old rocking chair sat beside the bed flanked by a small smoking table with an ashtray and a well-used pipe.

A table and lamp near the windows displayed a picture of an old man and Rick Teater. I picked it up. I didn't know the old man, but somehow he seemed familiar. The face

suspended my pursuit for a few moments. I was drawn to it
for some reason, but I didn't know why. I shrugged and
continued my search. Some tattered old brown corduroy
shoes sat near the fireplace. Maybe one of Rick's relatives
had lived with him in the past.

I crept over to the bed and lifted the bed skirt. Nothing.
I glanced back at the picture. It gave me an eerie feeling. I
shook it off again and headed for the bathroom, a lovely
room with plain high gloss white floors, walls, and fixtures,
in sharp contrast to the adjoining bedroom. I reversed and
went back to the hall, checking huge closets as I went.

Another door led to Rick Teater's master suite. I had to
be getting close to the intruder, unless he had somehow
circled around behind me and given me the slip. I looked
back and saw nothing. I couldn't hear anything but howling
wind and rain beating on the windows.

I worked my way around the bedroom, cautiously
opening every door. I glimpsed something out of the corner
of my eye. Rapidly I ducked around the corner, my revolver
ready. Perspiration beaded in the bend of my elbow. I
listened, but still couldn't distinguish a sound over the wailing
wind and rain.

I craned my head around the corner and pulled back
again. Movement. I inhaled deeply and swung my body
around into the room, coming face-to-face with my own
image in the mirror. The hair on my body bristled. I raggedly
exhaled.

On my way back across the bedroom, I checked under
the bed. Nobody. The huge walk-in closet full of expensive
suits and fine beachwear offered nothing unusual.

Next I headed to the door across from the master suite.
I put my ear to the door, thinking I heard a noise, like a
groan. I put my finger on the trigger and carefully turned
the knob.

An overturned vase of dead flowers spilled across a beautiful oriental rug. I swung around to the front of a massive mahogany desk near the window. Next to the wall-to-wall bookcases sat two large brown leather chairs, but no Lincoln Tumu. I walked over to the desk and caught a whiff of fish odor in the trashcan—boiled shrimp and cocktail sauce, way past its prime. So who'd left this mess?

Suddenly a knife zipped by my eyes as my shoulder was clawed. The intruder put the blade against my neck, and I felt a sting the instant I elbowed him hard in the chest.

I turned as Tumu dropped the knife, ran out of the room and across the hall, jumped off the master suite balcony, and escaped down the beach, leaving a massive window open to the elements. I looked down at blood covering my shirt and put my hand to my neck.

He got me. But how bad?

At that moment I heard voices from downstairs. Did Tumu have an accomplice who'd finish me off? I eased back into the hall and worked my way to the stairs, gun gripped tightly in my fist until I recognized the voice before I reached its owner. Charlie and Max stared. "How did you know my location?" I asked, flipping on the light switch.

"My God, Logan! What the hell happened?" Charlie grabbed me by the arm. I wavered, and Max set me down on the step, wrapping his jacket around my neck.

"Linc. He was in Teater's office, making himself at home. He surprised me with a knife. How bad?" I asked, pulling down my collar so they could look.

"Uh, hard to say. I'll take you to Urgent Care."

"Damn it, did you see him? Did you see Linc leaving? He jumped off the balcony up there and ran down to the beach. He oughtta be hurt but he didn't look it."

"Sorry, Logan. I guess we'd come around to the front by then. We never saw him. While we were checking each house and keeping up with the weather, we spotted the top of your Beemer. Put two and two together. You scared the crap outta me. Don't ever go out on your own that way again. I want to know where you are every minute, young lady." Charlie spoke in a sharp tone.

"Max, get after Tumu. He's bound to leave tracks in this weather. Call those same guys from the mainland if you have to. I'm taking Logan outta here." Max pulled his pistol and headed toward the beach. I told Charlie my radio was worthless and that I had tried to call. He promised me a new one.

Outside, the storm's heavy rain eased a bit. And the strong wind actually felt good on my body, now sweating profusely. The sting on my neck had turned into a throb.

"Well, the only good thing I can say about the storm is that it's leaving in a hurry," Charlie muttered, trying to get my mind off the cut, I suppose. "Let's get you doctored up. Are you sure you're okay?"

"I'll be fine. I'll just drive my Beemer and follow you," I replied.

"Oh, umm…about your car…" stammered Charlie.

"What's wrong with my car?"

"You won't be driving it anymore, Logan." I ran around the house to the gazebo and stopped at the top of the path, just making out the top of my old friend, completely covered with ocean water, a victim of stupidity. I teared up and stared. Charlie gave my arm a tug.

"I should've known better," I moaned. "It never occurred to me—"

"High tide on top of the storm. You should have parked farther away from the ocean. Someone'll have to dig it out once the storm is completely over. I'm afraid I don't have another squad car to loan you. Come on, I'll give you a lift to the doctor. We'll figure this out later."

"Charlie, there's a big window open in the master suite."

"I'll run up there and close it. Get in the car." I obeyed.

Charlie took me by Urgent Care and they cleaned up the cut and stitched me up. Linc had missed my jugular vein but I'd have a nasty scar. I knew I was lucky. Nobody had to say it. And I was hungry and shaken. I couldn't remember the last time I'd eaten. Charlie took me out to eat, but we had little to say except for his continuous scolding. I was still tense. I only picked at my food, nausea setting in on top of everything else. Then the chief drove me home and said he and Max would continue to search for Linc, but I needed to rest. I didn't argue.

Once at home and locked in, I called Doug, a friend of mine who owned a car dealership and a few rentals. I told him my dilemma, and he promised to have a car sitting outside my house the next morning with the key in it. I could keep it as long as I needed to.

Lexus came running to me, half-starved. What I was doing was so unfair to her. I had to remember to leave the commode seat up with fresh water, and to make certain she had enough food in her dish for at least twenty-four hours, since this case took all my time. I went to the kitchen and poured her food before running the water for a hot bubble bath.

Steamy citrus mist filled the room. I hoped it would relax me. I banged my fist on the tub, upset Lincoln Tumu was still at large. He could be anywhere by now. I didn't want my first case to end this way. My mind was too full of muck to unwind, but at least I'd be clean.

After my bath, I checked the answering machine, but there was only a hang-up. I hadn't yet invested in Caller ID so I had no idea who'd called. Might have been my mother, who hated leaving messages on machines. Charlie would have left a message. Even though it was early, I was too tired and sore to get into any intense conversations. I thought about Pepper Ellis again. Having to take full responsibility for Rick's funeral had to be another heartache for her.

15

This time the long-fingered bony hand grabbed my arm and I screamed, jolting up from the bed with my heart racing. I couldn't catch my breath. I snatched at my gown and gasped for air. I pulled the gown over my head, thinking my heart would burst.

Breathe in, breathe out, breathe in, breathe out. Calm down.

I gradually began to move my feet, and walked in a circle for a few minutes.

That was too real.

The nightmare was getting worse. I still couldn't remember anything but the hand.

Whose hand is it? Why is it after me?

16

The next morning I walked out to find a car sitting in front of my place: a clunky old Pontiac Firebird, more than likely held together by rust. Another nightmare, but I wasn't going to complain. It had stick shift, and I had trouble getting it to change gears as I backed out and started down the road. The Firebird spit and sputtered, making it difficult to handle.

The tropical storm just grazed the North Carolina coast. Not too much damage other than overturned trashcans and small yard decorations up and down the streets, and substantial beach erosion at the shoreline. The road was strewn with small tree limbs and many tufts of sea grass that dislodged from the dunes. The corner Amoco station lost its top-heavy roof and a few panes of glass. Almost all houses off the beach seemed to be fine except for yard debris. Even Genesis Golf and Country Club seemed spared major damage; it would just need to dry out. We were very lucky.

TideLand didn't seem damaged either, except for plenty of sand blown all around the pool and patio, one tree that fell away from the house, and the door window broken by

Linc. Losing my Beemer—pure stupidity on my part—couldn't be blamed on the storm alone.

My re-charged cell phone rang. Charlie said to get to the station as fast as I could and hung up. I gunned the gas pedal and the old car sputtered off toward the station. Charlie and Max were outside talking with two county deputies, and motioned me to Charlie's police car.

"Ken over at the grocery store said he spotted a man going through the Dumpster. Matched Linc's description."

I held on as Charlie skidded his cruiser around the corner and into the Hop'n Shop parking lot. Ken McAllister stood near the back of the store waiting for us. Deputies on loan from mainland stations pulled in beside us.

McAllister showed us the Dumpster. "He saw me looking at him and ran off through that tall brush over yonder and out to that other street," Ken said, pointing. We showed him a picture of Linc. "I'm pretty sure it was him, even though he looked much worse than his picture. He stuffed things in his pocket and took off on foot." He handed the picture back to Charlie.

We thanked him and looked around. One deputy walked out through the brush to see if it lay down where the person had run. It hadn't. We searched every home and business near the grocery store until late afternoon and came up empty.

Frustration and fatigue plagued all of us. Once we got back to the station, Charlie ordered me to go home and said he'd assign twenty-four-hour shifts, letting Max take the first shift. I nodded, but I wasn't going home.

17

I made sure Linc hadn't doubled back to the old house, then put my gun away and pulled some steel-tipped heavy-duty gloves out of my pocket. I decided to start at the door and work my way around. I picked up objects and put them back down. I'm not sure what I was looking for. As I passed the bathroom door, the smell of urine nauseated me. A peek into the room confirmed it hadn't been cleaned in months.

Cheap striped socks were strewn everywhere. I started a pile of them near the right side of the door, hoping to find the odd sock that matched the one found at the crime scene. I spotted traces of white powder too. I flipped open a zip-lock bag and raked it inside. I reached for an old newspaper and found it wrapped around three drug pipes, a pack of razor blades, and a small mirror. Pulling out another baggie, I dropped each item inside before sealing and labeling it. I reached the kitchen door, finding it as nasty as the bathroom.

I stepped back across the threshold and reached for another sock, snatching it from under a Styrofoam food carton. It was heavy, something lumpy in it. I went to the wood table I'd cleared, peered inside the bag, and poured its contents onto the table—two rounds of Cor bath soap, badly deformed.

The kind of soap Rick Teater used.

I recalled a Criminal Justice classroom scenario about an inmate who beat a man to death with a soap sock and it didn't leave any external bruises. I dialed the crime lab in Raleigh and told Malcolm Bryant my theory, and that I might be holding the murder weapon in my hand. He thought so too.

I radioed Charlie to tell him what I'd found. He was pleased and not surprised I hadn't gone home. This new discovery put Linc at the murder scene and added more evidence to go with the footprints. The chief wanted this new evidence to go to the lab immediately. He said a deputy went to Maury, a minimum-security prison, to get the details of a year-old murder committed by Linc's uncle, an inmate. "Linc's uncle beat a fellow prisoner to death with a soap sock. It didn't leave any bruises on the body, and he would have gotten away with it, except he bragged about it. Apparently Linc heard about it too."

"Maybe that's the same case we talked about in one of my classes."

"Probably."

I headed for the station with the soap sock, drug bags, and renewed enthusiasm about the investigation.

18

I drove my old Firebird rental to Pepper Ellis's condo and pulled into the driveway behind her black Fiat. I got out and walked toward the stairs before noticing her sitting in the car. She saw me and opened the door, her eyes still red and swollen.

"You look awful," she said as our eyes met.

"Uh, I just wanted to check on you. I have no ulterior motive, Ms Ellis."

"What happened to you?"

"I had a little run-in with a suspect."

"A suspect in Rick's murder?"

I nodded, touching my bandaged neck. She stepped out of the Fiat and I let her pass.

"Come on in with me."

We walked up the stairs to her door in silence. She headed off to the kitchen, kicking off her black heels. The sophisticated black dress adorned only by a beige silk flower pin hung on her lithe body. I wondered how much weight she'd lost in the few days since I'd met her.

She tossed her sunglasses on the kitchen table and headed for the refrigerator. "Wine? I have some Scuppernong Blush from The Duplin Winery."

"Sure, sounds like just what I need," I replied, finding a stool at the antique island. She got two flutes, poured the wine, and pulled out aged Canadian white cheddar.

"Let me change out of these funeral clothes first." She managed a sad smile. "I'll cook us up something while we talk. Please don't object, Agent Hunter. I need the company," she said before I could respond.

I watched her go around the corner toward her bedroom, reached for some crackers, and cut a thin slice of cheese to go with my wine. I sipped on my second serving as she emerged barefoot, revealing ten perfect toes.

"I hope you don't mind my helping myself to another glass. It's delicious."

"Oh, by all means, help yourself. I buy it by the case."

"I'm sorry I had to miss the funeral. But I guess my time was well spent. How did it go?" I asked, looking into the saddest face I'd ever seen.

She shrugged. "How well can any funeral go? Many people were there, but no family. I sat there thinking that even though Rick was wealthy, he was needy in some ways. I think he would've given up his millions to have a family. He wasn't the person people made him out to be. He seldom used drugs, and not at all as long as I've known him. He wouldn't even take aspirin, for Pete's sake! He never had any wild parties. He may have when he was younger, but at fifty-five, I think he was ready to settle down. He had his share of regrets, like never having children. He was adamant about no drugs in the house. He was a kind and gentle man, Agent Hunter."

She sighed and drank her wine. I let her finish and lead the conversation. "He taught me how to swim, you know. I was always scared of the water. My brother used to try to dunk me, and I always ended up with a mouth full of water, gasping for air. Rick was patient and never made fun of me. He used to accuse me of sinking to get him to rush to me and lift me up. I really think it was lack of confidence on my part though."

Her eyes filled with tears and she grabbed a tissue from the kitchen counter. "I just can't believe it's all over. I've tried to remember every word we said to each other over the past few months. I guess I didn't pay enough attention. He told me several stories about his childhood, and how he started what he called his 'tub and stub' business. He was smart even though he never went to college. His common sense approach to just about everything fascinated me.

"He moved around a lot growing up. His dad was a preacher. I thought he died several years ago, but I heard today he's still living, if you want to call it that. Rick's mother developed cancer and died shortly after diagnosis years ago. He was an only child. He never married. I guess he enjoyed the bachelor life too much to settle down.

"He had plenty of friends, although sometimes he wasn't sure if they were really friends or just enjoyed spending his money. His father even lived with him for a few months until he had to go to a nursing home. I understand he's somewhere around Norfolk, but I'm not sure the reason for that location. He and Rick didn't get along very well, but Rick tried to do his duty as a son. His dad didn't come to the funeral. I doubt he even knows Rick is gone."

We both shifted and reached for more cheese.

"How did you meet him, Miss Ellis?"

"I met him in Wilmington. Not Mr. Teater, but Rick. He and his old high school friend, Andy, ordered spinach pizza in the restaurant where I was the head cook. This gorgeous man winked at me, and I blushed, and started making a large spinach pizza and delivered it to the table myself. After a couple of slices, I could tell they were impressed. They devoured the whole thing, making loud obnoxious compliments so I could hear them. I had to laugh.

"Rick gave me his business card and said to please call him. I really need to call Andy. He lives in Hawaii now. I never thought of calling him. I should have. I dread that." I waited for her to move through these new emotions without my interference.

The chef leaned over the island, smiling faintly at me. "I'm sorry to let this all out on you."

"It's okay."

"Place your order, ma'am," she said, lightly slapping the island with the palm of her hand.

"Gosh, I have no idea. Surprise me."

She smiled and went to the refrigerator. "Well, we've had wine and cheese. Let's see what I can whip up. You aren't allergic to shellfish, are you?"

"No."

"I know you probably think I'm cold, Agent Hunter, but cooking is therapeutic. I'm sorry to rattle on. I haven't been able to talk to anyone. My family lives out west now. I've kept so much bottled up." She eased out a long sigh. "Anyway, I called the number on his business card: 'Rick Teater, Teater Pool and Spa International'. I didn't know he was a millionaire. Some lady answered the phone, and I told her I was a chef and Mr. Teater had asked me to call. I left my number.

"It was several days before he called. He'd been out of state on business. He asked me if I was a real chef, and I laughed and said 'full-fledged'. He said he'd be interested in hiring me to cater parties for him and cook occasional intimate dinners for guests.

"He asked me to come to his house. I wasn't sure where it was. I lived in Wilmington then, not Genesis Beach. He gave me directions, and when I pulled up to the TideLand sign, it was unbelievable! I thought I was at the wrong place. The housekeeper, Akiko, answered the door and showed me into the kitchen. I almost wet my panties! It looked like a huge restaurant kitchen. Well, I'm sure you've seen it. I was completely awestruck. She said Mr. Teater would be in soon, to have a look around.

"I guess he gave me time to fall in love with the place before he came in. It worked. I think I'd have asked to cook for free. We talked and he asked for a trial week and wanted me to cater an event during that week. He gave me free rein on what to do, handing me a credit card to get everything from flowers to linens to food. I'd never had such an opportunity and so much fun."

Pepper had a radiant smile on her face. I enjoyed listening to her talk about her two passions, Rick Teater and cooking.

"Obviously people liked Rick; it wasn't just the money. He was a likeable guy, good to people. Generous, not snooty. Down-to-earth. Once people began to leave the party, I gathered up things and headed back to the kitchen to clean up. I was busy tidying up when I heard applause from the doorway. Rick stood there, looking gorgeous in white pants, a white shirt, partly unbuttoned, and white deck shoes. He asked me where I'd been all his life. He said the trial was over and he wanted to hire me on a permanent basis. I said 'Yes' before I could stop myself. He only had one other party, on the Fourth of July. A big bash—not wild, but sophisticated."

At the stove now, the chef sprinkled crabmeat onto the top of eggs she'd broken in the skillet, the smell divine. She thrust another bottle of chilled Duplin wine toward me, and I slid two fresh goblets from the under-counter rack.

"At first Rick asked for only a few meals a week. He was gone a lot. He gradually stayed home more and wanted me to cook almost every night. He seldom ate leftovers, so I took them home or gave them to his housekeeper, Akiko. One night he invited a lady over, and she called late in the afternoon to say she couldn't make it. He asked me to cook the meal anyway and be his date. I felt awkward, but he insisted. So once dinner was ready, I sat down across from him and we enjoyed the meal and each other's company.

"After the meal, he put his arms around me and asked me to stay all night. I said 'No' and worked myself out of his grip. He asked me why, and I told him I was uncomfortable doing that. He was a rich playboy, and I a country bumpkin. He laughed and walked to the kitchen door.

"He turned around with a serious look on his face. 'I didn't mean to scare you,' he said. I could feel my skin getting hot and turning red. I continued to clean up and heard him walking down the hall. I wanted to run after him, but I forced myself to finish cleaning up, and then I left.

"After a few weeks of this same routine, I finally gave in and stayed. I have to admit I was smitten. Anyway, the guests had stopped coming and the dates seemed to have ended. Rick came home just about every night, expecting dinner and a few drinks—a regular house puppy. It seemed to suit him. He was happy and content. I hope I was the reason for that." Pepper Ellis had wound down and looked tired now.

"How well did you know Akiko?"

"Not well at all. She seemed to work around my schedule, usually coming when I wasn't there. She kept the place spotless though. She seemed rather aloof to me, but Rick said she just wasn't comfortable having another woman in the house on a regular basis."

We sat there a few minutes in silence before she clicked on the TV remote. The weather came on as she changed the channel. "Wait," I requested. "Go back. Did he say something about a hurricane?"

She flipped back to the station just in time to get the satellite picture of a threatening hurricane out in the Atlantic, its outer bands only hours away, but already a full-blown hurricane and heading straight for our coastline.

"A storm is still to our east, now considered extra-tropical. However, a Category Four hurricane is heading west, and will turn north up the Carolina coast, thanks in part to the tropical storm remnants. North Carolina coastal residents should pay close attention." I cringed. That little storm remnant we'd had earlier didn't compare to a Category Four hurricane.

Pepper Ellis shoved a magnificent crabmeat omelet at me as the phone rang. She walked into another room, but I could hear her gasping. I stayed put, looking at the omelet with delight. I hoped this call wasn't more bad news. She returned, still holding the phone in her hand.

"What's wrong?" I asked. All the color had drained from her face. She handed me the phone and sat down. I waited while she buried her head in her hands before looking up into my eyes.

"It's Rick's..." she muttered. "That was Rick's attorney, the executor of his estate." The chef gulped and fought back the tears. "Rick made me the beneficiary of his entire estate. Oh, my God, what does this mean?" The woman grabbed both my arms. "What's it mean?"

I gently put my arms around hers. "I think it means Rick loved you."

"But he wouldn't have..."

"You said yourself he had no family except his incapacitated dad. You obviously meant more to him than anyone else." We sat quietly for a few more minutes before she stared at me in alarm.

"But it makes me look guilty again. Motive, right?" She looked panicked.

"Well, er...no, there's still more than one suspect."

"But I'm one of them. And I've babbled on about my life with Rick. That's why you came here, isn't it? To take advantage of me. This is all so incredible. I don't know what to do."

"No, I didn't come here to take advantage, Ms. Ellis. I'm concerned about you. That's all. You're in shock, and this is another shock, although a good one." I cleared my throat. "I should go now. I'm sorry if my coming here upset you. That was so not my intention. After all, you're the one who asked me to stay."

She guzzled her wine. "Wait. Don't go. I'm sorry. Just don't go yet." She went to the kitchen pantry and came back with a liter of wine, pouring herself another one and topping off mine. "Some things I can't do anything about. I did love Rick. I had no idea he'd made me beneficiary. Agent Hunter, I swear to you, I didn't kill him."

The chef leaned over the island and motioned me to the living room. I reluctantly carried my plate and wine glass, and she brought hers along with the rest of the wine. We sank into the sofa. I threw her a napkin and started to recap all the events of the investigation.

"Ms Ellis, I need to tell you a few things you may not know about Rick. I've been digging into his background. You know, to see if he had enemies. I've talked to old friends and business partners he had over the years." She bristled. "He did have enemies. Not everybody liked Rick. He had quite a few enemies, in fact, especially in business. He undercut some folks on his way up the success ladder, and there are people who probably had it in for him. Particularly Seth Walker and R.C. Houser."

"Who? I've never heard of them."

"Well, Walker and Houser owned the place where Rick worked when he was in his twenties. A regular garden tub place. Rick, being the entrepreneur, took that idea outside and created the hot tub spa rage people still love. Then he pumped it up a notch to the thermal spa."

"So what's wrong with that? Did Rick do something illegal?"

"No. He just pissed them off because he had the idea and they didn't. I'm not saying he was wrong. But people hold grudges, regardless." She understood. "And there were a couple of women, I understand, who wanted to castrate him because he wasn't faithful. And then there were the drug parties." The chef waved her hand for me to stop.

"Look, I know Rick was no saint. But most of that stuff was years ago. Before I met him. He outgrew it. Especially the drugs. He came to loathe them, like I already told you. I'm telling you he was a different man. He despised gays though, and paid some off to keep them from opening a gay tavern on the beach."

"Do you know any names? Anybody who'd be mad enough to go after Rick?" She shook her head.

I told her Rick hadn't cheated on her, and her face lit up momentarily. I mentioned that Chyna heard Rick say the word 'pepper', and I knew he was referring to her even though he was drugged. She put her plate down and began to cry. I'd said enough. It was late into the night, and we were both exhausted. I walked to the door and let myself out, my head swimming in wine.

The wind gusted and a sizable tree limb came out of nowhere and hit the side of my car. I decided to go straight home, get inside, and find out more about this storm. Damn it! Finding Linc was the top priority, and I wasn't psyched for another storm right now. I prayed for it to move on past us, or at least weaken considerably. If it didn't, we'd be up Shit Creek.

19

I looked out the window toward the southeast. Another nightmare had destroyed any possibility of rest. This time I saw the hand coming and ran from it, literally getting out of bed and sleepwalking over to the door in the middle of the night. I managed to get it unlocked, and only woke up when the wind hit my face. I climbed back under the covers, my eyes wild and wide open.

The sky was sinister. Wind rocked the old house, and I rolled out of bed and yawned my way into the kitchen to make some strong coffee. Then I flopped across the covers I'd kicked loose in the throes of terror to scratch Lexus's ears. She clung to me this morning, wanting me to comfort her. She was my comfort too. The only comfort I had.

If only Linc were in custody I could lounge around all day. But since duty called, I showered and sat down at the bistro table to watch the angry ocean. The surf was above normal as waves raced each other, some crashing on top of others onshore. Seagull squeaks, normally calming, were now nerve-racking. A few surfers emerged to tackle the elevated waves, seldom this high unless there was a hurricane nearby.

I dressed in khaki shorts and a black tee shirt since the humidity was thick enough to spoon into a cereal bowl. I towel-dried my hair even though it would be wet with perspiration before I got to work.

On my way to the station I saw several pickup trucks with plywood, the people inside boarding up their property to prevent as much damage as possible. I walked into the office and literally ran into Maggie, leaving to weatherproof her own house.

"What's that smell?" I asked with upturned nose.

"Oh, Oi had to spray. One of tha fellers had a colon cleansin' in tha bathroom and my delicate system just couldn't take it, not with tha storm nerves Oi've got. Tha storm's coming in at hoi toide, and that's not good. Be safe, Logan." Maggie shook her head and disappeared.

I dialed Charlie and he told me to go back home but to take the long way and make sure houses and businesses looked secure, not to stay out too long, and to be safe. He'd call me if he needed me, he promised. I rode the beach, but didn't find anything suspicious, only men hammering plywood over vulnerable glass. I picked up beach balls and stacked a few abandoned plastic chairs and hauled them over the dune, trying to push them under a deck step where they might survive with any luck.

I pulled into my driveway, surveying what might need to be moved inside the old house or tied down. The wind beat mama's old faded rooster flag, so I walked over to it, loosened the pole, and wrestled it and the flag inside with me. I grabbed a few large potted plants my mother had kept alive for years and set them on the bay windowsill before walking out on the back deck, taking the umbrella out of the center of the glass table, turning the table on its side, and rolling it into the corner to lay flat. I dragged the two Carolina blue porch rockers inside.

Once all the windows were secured, I put towels around the bottom of each one to confine any water that might blow in. I'd been through many hurricanes in my life, but not completely alone.

Maybe I should leave in the morning. I packed valuables as tight as possible in the closet and slammed the door quickly to keep everything from tumbling out.

I strolled around the house picking up sentimental treasures and sailing off into my memories. My daddy's railroad clock was there on the wall, given to him when the Atlantic Coastline depot, where he was agent, closed forever. The octagonal face with Roman numerals was still in good shape. The hands had to be cranked every thirty days. The brass pendulum swung and tick tocked just enough to be relaxing. It didn't have an obnoxious noise—no binging or bonging, and no fake bird tweeting. I loved it. I could remember Daddy putting a jar lid of kerosene under the pendulum occasionally to keep the movements working. It was time I did that. I slowly cranked it and closed its antique glass doors gently.

I touched two of my mother's oil paintings as I passed. She was so talented, and I couldn't draw a circle or a straight line. My favorite one of the ninety-nine she'd painted was a naked girl sitting on a pier with her black Lab beside her. Total innocence. Total contentment. Me, at eight, with my hair pinned into a messy wad on top of my head with Choo Choo, the only dog I'd ever owned.

I headed for the small brick fireplace and glanced over it at my daddy's fly rod. Before his death, fishing had been one of his favorite hobbies. He'd always said he'd grow roses when he retired although a sudden massive heart attack ended that dream. I straightened the rod with a gentle touch.

I shoved a bag of popcorn in the microwave, turned on the TV, and curled up on the sofa with Lexus. In minutes I nodded off. I'm not sure how long I slept, but I awoke to a noise outside in the darkness.

I recognized Charlie's voice and ran to the door in time to see Charlie and Max drive by, announcing a voluntary evacuation of the beach over a loudspeaker. I ran out the door and flagged down the police car moving down the street at parade pace.

"Charlie! Where is it?" I hollered across Max.

"It's right off the South Carolina coast, coming right at us. It's picked up a lot of speed. The first bands will be here in a couple of hours. Landfall is supposed to be around Cape Fear. They're saying it'll weaken then. If it doesn't, we'll be wiped out. The storm surge alone will take out many surf houses. I decided not to call you in on this one, Logan. Max and I'll handle the warning. Just take care of your property and yourself. I'd suggest you head inland. You need to leave now. I wish we had Tumu in custody. Every hour makes it more likely he got off the beach somehow. We have an APB on him in the Carolinas and Virginia. That's all we can do. Anyway, we gotta go. Be safe." The car began to move forward; I stepped aside and waved.

I was nervous about this old house, built before mandatory hurricane specs. I hoped it was built high enough to get little water damage. If the wind damaged the roof, the house would flood anyway, but I couldn't do much about it.

I stepped over to my closest neighbor's house. Jack Norton said he'd board up my surfside windows and patio doors, and told me he and his family were staying. I thanked him and headed inside to make a decision.

The phone rang. "Agent Hunter? This is Pepper Ellis. Are you staying through the hurricane?"

"Yeah, I guess. I really don't have anywhere to go. My neighbor's boarding up for me, though. Nice, huh?"

"Sure is. I guess I need to go over to TideLand and make sure it can withstand the storm. Since I'm on the sound, I think my place'll be safe. I know you said you live on the ocean. You're welcome to come and stay with me. In fact, I wish you would. I can't bear to think of being here alone right now. I'm going to cook a few recipes I haven't tried in a while, and I need a taster."

"Thank you. I'll think about it. When are you going to the estate? I can go with you if you need help getting things inside and checking all those windows. I've done about all I know to do here."

"We'd better go now. I'll swing by and pick you up." She paused. "By the way, where do you live?"

I told her how to get to my place and decided maybe off the beach would be better than on the beach. This storm, according to the nearest TV station, would come ashore at high tide with winds over one hundred miles per hour in total darkness, but at least it was no longer a Cat Four. I rechecked the forecast, and the landfall prediction had moved farther north, very close to Genesis Beach, and we would get the strongest quadrant of the storm. My skin whelped with goose pimples at the thought.

I'd have to do something with Lexus. I couldn't go off and leave her here alone. She'd be petrified of the wind, or she might be hurt. She sat at my feet, looking up at me with those gorgeous blueberry eyes. I called Jack next door. He had a cat, and I'd kept her for him before, but not in this kind of weather. I asked him if he would keep Lexus, and he said he would since she's an inside cat anyway, to bring her food, and he would take care of the rest. That reply made my decision to pack a small bag and go home with Pepper Ellis after we went to Rick's estate.

I put my gray hooded parka on the counter by the door, gathered up a sleepy Lexus, got her Deli Cat, and went over to Jack's.

"You're such a good neighbor. I'll have to do something special for you," I said.

"Oh, please. Your mother did so many favors for us, it's about time we reciprocated. Don't worry about it. I've got you boarded up except the patio doors, and I'll do that in a few minutes. Lexus'll be safe. You take care of yourself." Janet, Jack's wife, came to greet Lexus. I wondered if she'd insisted on Jack saying 'Yes' because she had quickly fallen in love with Lexus. I kissed the furry head as she went to Janet, and I handed Jack the food. I promised to check on her, and, hopefully, pick her up tomorrow. I felt a pang of guilt for going off and leaving her, but I knew she'd be safe and somewhat content with Gabby, their cat.

I found my overnight bag and threw some underwear in, grabbed my toothbrush, basic makeup, and a few sets of clothing before I heard the Fiat horn blow. With one last look around, I grabbed Daddy's fly rod and Mama's favorite painting, locked the door, and left. I'd parked the rental car as close to the house as possible in hopes it wouldn't be damaged. I ran to the Fiat, threw my stuff in the back, tucked the fly rod behind the seat, and sat down beside Pepper.

The wind howled, and she had difficulty driving to the mansion. The Fiat shook us up considerably, and some debris hit us hard on its formidable trek to somewhere else. Every tall tree looked as if it would snap off at any minute. We were both getting scared. We pulled into the TideLand drive and Pepper drove around to the garage, getting as close to the door as possible.

"The alarm has to be cut off back here, if it's even on. Rick seldom used it, although his insurance agent chewed him out several times for not setting it. About the only time he'd set it was when he knew he was going to be gone over night. He never set it when he was home. Too trusting, I guess," she said. I remained silent. Pepper hopped out and ran to the garage side door and let herself in, turning on the lights. A few seconds later the garage door opened and she ran back to the car and pulled it inside, squeezing it between

Rick's Infiniti QX56 and his Maserati convertible with the top still down.

"After I get you inside, I'd better put the top up, if I can find the keys. And I'll turn on the floodlights outside," Pepper reasoned. We managed to crawl out of the Fiat and inch our way to the back door. I hadn't been in this area of the house. Teater had four vehicles in this garage, including an awesome copper-colored Hummer and a Harley-Davidson that looked like sterling silver. Pepper said the Bentley was stored elsewhere.

We went into the hallway and saw the broken pane in the back door.

"I'll find something to cover," I told her as she grabbed a key and ran back to put the convertible top up. It was already raining in on the floor so I got a towel from the wooden bench, wiped up the water, and left the towel on the floor. I decided to move the plants from around the pool, dragging a heavy potted palm up under the arbor and jogging back for another one.

Pepper joined me and together we lifted the rest of the plants and trees and got them to the arbor. Once we moved all the plants to safety, I picked up yard statues I could lift, and Pepper folded a long table and dragged it to the house. We surveyed our work and decided we'd done all we could do.

The blustery weather made it tough to stand, the sky ominous to the southeast. We didn't have much time left. We headed inside, and Pepper hesitated at the stairs.

"Will you take care of the upstairs while I do the downstairs?"

I bolted up the stairs, turning on lights as I went through each room checking the windows with no time to straighten the flower mess I'd forgotten about in Rick's office. Someone would have to clean that after the storm.

I finished upstairs almost in a run. Rain and wind battered the windows. Something went by them that resembled dirty laundry suds. Sea foam. Not a good sign especially this high on a hill. I flew down the stairs and found Pepper sitting on the kitchen floor.

"We've got to get out unless you want to spend the hurricane here." She wiped a tear and nodded, lifting her hands. I pulled her up, and we sprinted toward the garage. I ran to the bathroom nearest the hot tub and found a small freestanding cupboard. I dragged it over to put in front of the door with the broken pane, turned off the lights, locked the door, and closed it behind me.

"I guess we've been through enough together that you can call me Pepper," she smiled.

Pepper raised the door and backed out. We took off at record speed down the driveway. She slowed down but didn't stop as she wrestled with the steering wheel in gusts that could turn us over. Folks with any sense were already battened down.

We worked our way through much more numerous tree limbs, and passed my house. I gave it a glance and all seemed well, except for some roof shingles flapping in the breeze. We headed for Pepper's condo. We had to cross water twice, storm surges coming over or between the sand dunes and across the road. I wondered if my old house could take it. And I worried about Lexus.

We shot into Pepper's driveway, and I grabbed my bag, pictures, and rod, and sprinted up the stairs behind Pepper, not letting the wind blow me over the railing.

"Wow! That's a storm!" Pepper almost yelled. I put my bag down near the kitchen door. We crashed on the peppermint-striped couch and flipped on the TV to get the latest storm coordinates, both breathing hard.

"If the electricity goes off, I have a generator, but I'm not sure I know how to use it. Rick insisted I have one after that storm last summer knocked out the power for a week. Remember?" I did. This storm was supposed to be worse. I shuddered.

20

Pepper walked me to her extra bedroom, flipping on lights and showing me where to put my things and freshen up. I looked out the bedroom window and could see the few trees bowing and swaying uncontrollably. I didn't see how they could withstand much more.

I looked at myself in the mirror and had to smirk at my hair standing up in stiff peaks around the top of my head. I tried to flatten it out, but it didn't want to settle down. Bags of dark flesh noticeable under each eye begged for restful sleep. I ran my fingers across my throat, healing well, and finally unbandaged but throbbing nevertheless. The double bed looked comfortable and inviting, although I had a feeling there wouldn't be much sleeping on this stormy night.

I found Pepper in the kitchen, pulling out a variety of ingredients from the refrigerator and the pantry shelves. She smiled when I walked in. "I need to do this. Therapy, you know." I nodded.

I could gain fifty pounds during this hurricane, but, hey, anything for a friend, right? A friend...that sounds nice.

"Call me Logan," I said unexpectedly. It just seemed the right time, and after all, she was letting me stay with her during a hurricane. Pepper smiled. "Don't you want to rest a while?"

"Rest? Are you crazy? Who could rest?" She had a point.

"What can I do to help?" She gave me a cooking tool assignment, and once I assembled the items, I sat down on a bar stool across the island from her.

"I'm about cried out. I feel so hollow inside. But I keep hearing Rick's voice. You know, Logan, he wanted me to pursue my dreams. He's told me so many times to open my own restaurant. I told him I didn't have the desire needed to cook twenty-four/seven and I refused investment money from him. Now I think I have the resolve. I don't know how to explain it. It's like I've been inspired, or I owe him, I suppose. Anyhow, I have to do it. Open my own restaurant, I mean. I want to bury myself in food. Maybe when I see people enjoying it, I'll see Rick's face, his smile. Crazy, huh?" Pepper plopped down on a stool.

"No, I don't think it's crazy at all. It sounds exciting. And I'm glad you have a positive attitude about all this. Any ideas on where the restaurant will be?"

"Probably Raleigh or Charlotte. Maybe even Asheville, but certainly not here. I mean, I love this place, but these folks generally want barbecue and plain country food like collards. Chefs cook more flamboyant meals that are highly creative and artistic. I wouldn't be able to make a living here. The only way I kept my head above water before Rick hired me was my catering business. Weddings, special corporate luncheons, and such. We don't have many corporations around here either, and beach weddings are few and far between."

When we went into the den I sat on the floor and started stretching and contorting. Pepper joined me. "Teach me a few moves. You know, SBI stuff."

"I'm just stretching right now. Do this with me, and then I'll show you a coupla moves." We stretched and I did two hundred sit-ups while Pepper did ten and counted for me. "Wow. There's no way I could do that," she said.

"It takes time and discipline." I stretched and started jacks while she jumped in for a few.

"I'm totally out of shape. I need to do this every day."

"It's a good stress buster too," I chimed in. "But we're both too tired for this right now."

The wind howled and the condo quivered. We hunkered down and talked for hours, helping ease the tension we both felt. "Logan, as sad as it makes me, going to Rick's today made me realize I can't stay there. If I sell the estate I should be able to open a fine place without starting out in debt up to my eyebrows. I couldn't bear to live at Tideland. Maybe I can get a lot for it if this storm doesn't do major damage," Pepper concluded.

I wandered over to the window. "Geez!" I noticed a piece of someone's deck floating by in the near darkness, along with many sea grass knots from dismantling sand dunes.

"The tidal surge is coming our way," I called to Pepper, on her way to the front door to look at her Fiat.

Water passed under it, but it was still in place. She didn't have a garage to put it in. I wondered if my rental was still where I'd left it. Probably not, since it was right over the sand dune. If the dune washed away, the car would be flooded, or maybe even moved.

I called Jack, who confirmed that the dunes were disappearing, and the Weather Channel had just announced waves at twenty feet above normal. But the storm had picked up speed and wouldn't be as bad as first predicted.

The storm wasn't supposed to be a major rainmaker, but the wind and surf would do substantial damage. It was now completely dark. While I talked with Jack, his power went off. Ours was still on for the moment, but we knew it would go off soon and probably wouldn't be back for days.

Pepper located candles and a lighter while she could still see.

Soon she brought bowls over to the island. "Do you like pizza?" she asked.

I nodded.

"Good! You'll love summer pie then. But you've got to help me. We've gotta move fast or eat it raw. I need these things from the fridge: minced garlic, red bell pepper… get the baby spinach—I don't have any basil—one egg, the milk, and the mozzarella."

At the refrigerator I could see most things before I opened the glass door. She laughed at me trying to do a balancing act with all the ingredients, and ran to help before I dropped the egg. She grabbed two tomatoes from the wire basket over the sink and sliced them paper thin with the speed and agility of a buzz saw.

"You like spinach?"

"I do. But I hope you don't expect me to chop like that," I shuttered.

"No, I'll do that part since we can't get out to a doctor," she said. Laughter filled the house as we put the summer pie into a phyllo shell and popped it into the top oven.

"Set the timer for fifty minutes." I did. So far, so good. We still had power. Pepper went into the living room and lit an array of colorful scented candles and a brass lantern. I followed her to the bedroom I used and lit two smaller vanilla candles before heading to Pepper's bedroom, where she converted the electric beaded lamps on each side of her embroidered headboard into candleholders. She inserted candles and lit them.

We headed back to the kitchen to start Apple Napoleons. This time I fetched the pastry dough from the freezer compartment of the large refrigerator. Pepper reached for four Granny Smiths and peeled each in one long curl. It was fascinating to watch how swiftly she cut. I wondered how many Band-aids it took to get so good.

The timer went off, and Pepper ran to get the summer pie. It had the most divine aroma—the smell of tomato and cheese zipping through the kitchen and into the living room. I liked these double ovens too. This kitchen had to be a chef's dream. She probably designed it herself.

Cinnamon took over the air space occupied by tomato and cheese. My tummy growled in anticipation. We worked fast, and Pepper put the apples on the gas stove to cook until tender. I got two plates and forks while Pepper grabbed a couple of napkins and two beers from the refrigerator.

"Tomato dishes need alcohol to awaken them," she explained with a grin. We moved to the oak table and dug in to the summer pie. Each flavor surfaced. Pepper was right; even though I didn't much care for beer, it was wonderful with this pie. We gorged ourselves and groaned with full tummies as the lights went out, leaving us in candlelight to listen to the constant roar of the hurricane.

"Never fear," Pepper whispered. "I have the apples on the gas stove. And I reckon they're about ready. I'm sure the pastry is too." She went to the stove and grabbed the stainless steel pot off the burner. "The apples have to cool or they'll melt the whipped cream."

We could hear the wind howling, and we both wished we could see outside. Storms that come through during the night are always more scary. I reached for my cell phone and called Jack again. He said everything was fine, not to worry. He would check things out once the storm passed. I thanked him and told him I wouldn't call again but to call me if he needed to.

Pepper retrieved whipped cream she'd made earlier in the day. As soon as the apples cooled, she began to demonstrate how to assemble an Apple Napoleon, laying the cooled pastry down and placing a huge dollop of whipped cream in its center. She placed cooked apple slices in a haystack formation around the cream. "Ta dah! Well, I have mine, now you make yours," she laughed, running into the living room and leaving me to try it on my own.

I laid a piece of pastry on the dish, scooped up some cream, and put it near the center. I started to place pieces of apple around, but they wanted to fall into the cream. Obviously there was a trick to making an apple haystack. She made it all look so easy. When I walked into the living room with my train wreck, she cackled and fell over on the sofa. I sat down on the white chair with my dessert, giggling too. I put my feet up on the rattan ottoman and got comfortable in the candlelight.

"I'll show you how to make it work after you finish eating. It'll still be good even though it won't win any beauty contest," Pepper teased and winked. We giggled again, and I inhaled my dessert. Pepper had already finished hers. We sat, listening to the storm, wind gusts shaking the condo steadily. With our appetites satisfied, both Pepper and I fell asleep.

I awoke first and walked softly across the floor to the back door. The wind didn't seem to be as strong, but the power appeared to be out all over the beach. We were in total darkness. Pepper uncurled from the sofa when I came back to the doorway. She stretched and asked how it looked outside.

"Too dark to tell."

Pepper toddled off to the kitchen and got the wine from the bar. "This stuff is even better at room temperature." She smiled. I faintly returned the smile. I didn't want to drink any more alcohol. She offered me some, and I declined as she poured herself a small amount in a juice glass.

"So, Logan, I'm curious. How did you become an agent?" I settled myself on the floor at her feet and began my story.

"You have to remember I'm still an intern, not a certified agent, at least not yet. When I was in high school one of my dad's friends was murdered, and the case was never solved. It tore the little town apart. That's when everybody started locking up at night. None of us ever got over that. I often wondered why the investigators didn't do more. Of course, I had no way of knowing what was going on, but the murder intrigued me, and I developed theories of my own. I took a high school course through the community college and became fascinated with criminal investigation.

"I majored in Criminal Justice at East Carolina University and applied for the SBI internship. Out of fifty-five applicants, only five of us made it. I was supposed to do my internship in Greenville, but Mama had a stroke. I requested to be assigned here to be near her. It was easy since Charlie Weiss's brother is in SBI administration."

We sat for a while and listened to the storm batter the roof and sides of the condo, only moving when we heard a loud bumping noise at the front door. Pepper looked out her door's peephole and saw what appeared to be a part of a child's trampoline up against the door. Wind puffed under the door. I picked up a small rug, rolled it up, and crammed it into the space.

Back in the kitchen I watched Pepper fix me another Apple Napoleon. The haystack making takes patience, which I had little of. Her apple slices didn't fall into the cream. I took my fork and cut into the masterpiece. Pepper fixed her Napoleon, and we returned to the living room. I sat on the floor and she sat down beside me. She looked at me with softness in her eyes.

"You're a good investigator, Logan. You deserve a permanent SBI position. I wish you luck." She reached out and squeezed my hand. I smiled, even though I didn't feel like a good investigator when Tumu was still at large. We both climbed into chairs and stretched out for more restless dozing.

21

"Don't tell nobody nothin', little darlin'," the raspy voice whispered close to my ear. I jerked away, but the long bony hand grabbed me, and the long nasty green nails bit into the skin on my arm. I could feel hot breath in my hair as my earlobe was licked. I bit a finger and the hand released me. I screamed at the top of my lungs as I ran outside in a storm and could barely stand up. Something hit me in the face, but I continued to try to run. The hand—no, two hands now—shook me hard, and I fell to the ground.

I awoke to Pepper pulling at me, both being beaten by the storm's wrath and soaked by its rain. Pepper wrapped herself around me so I couldn't run anymore. I stared at her for a moment and then began to shake violently.

"Logan! My God! You scared me half to death. What is it? What the hell is going on?" I could only blink at her. She pulled me to my feet, and together we made the laborious trip back to safety.

Once inside, Pepper breathlessly told me I'd screamed out several times—a lot of nonsense—and the only words she made out were 'Stay away' and I bolted for the door, somehow unlocked it, and ran out into the storm. I'd been hit in the ear by flying debris, and I'd bitten her finger when she grabbed me.

We dried off and sat quietly for a while, Pepper watching me as she doctored the bite. I rocked on the floor and tried to recover, not being able to get Lincoln Tumu off my mind.

Is he out there in this storm? Is he a potential threat to us? Would he ever be seen again?

And this bony hand drove me mad. I wanted relief from the overwhelming feeling of impending terror I couldn't explain. I felt totally wiped out. And I'd stressed Pepper with my behavior. With nowhere to go, we both needed to calm down.

She walked into the kitchen, mopped up the water by the door, and fetched the Crown Royal and two glasses of ice. Over whiskey we tried to compose ourselves, even though the building quavered around us.

"I'm so sorry, Pepper. I've been having a terrible nightmare over and over. I don't know why, and I don't know what to do about it."

"You need to see a doctor, Logan," she said. I sat still as Pepper doctored my bleeding ear. Then she sat down beside me on the floor, wrapping a Band-Aid around her bite.

"A shrink?" I suddenly yelled. "Are you saying I need a shrink?"

"No. Well, okay…Logan, everybody needs some help now and then. You need to find out what's causing the nightmare so you can end it, don't you think?" Pepper said gently. We sat in silence for a few uncomfortable minutes. Maybe I did need some help, but I was in no mood to admit it or to discuss it further.

"You never told me how you got so interested in cooking," I began, wanting to lighten the mood, and hide my fear. Not of the storm as much as what I might learn by seeing a shrink.

As the wind continued to howl, Pepper began her own story. "I've cooked since I was big enough to reach the kitchen countertop. My parents both worked until five or after, Monday through Friday. Mama even insisted I plan menus for an entire week, make a grocery list, and make sure we had all the necessary ingredients in the house.

"Daddy did most of the grocery shopping and had to buy a lot of pepper. I was heavy-handed with it. That's how I got my nickname. It stuck so well that when I was old enough, I made it legal."

"What's your real name?"

"I'm not telling." Pepper shifted and continued. "We weren't rich, but with the help of my guidance counselor, I got into the School of Culinary Arts at Johnson and Wales in Charleston. I loved the town and didn't go home much. I met lots of great people, some chefs now in New York City or Europe."

"Did you ever think of going somewhere like that, or maybe California?"

"Nope," answered Pepper. "I guess I've never been quite as passionate about cooking as they were. But I'm more inspired since I met Rick. He seemed like a little kid, wanting to see what I could create next and then eating it with dramatic gusto. He would make the cutest faces and noises while he inhaled one of my creations," Pepper said, her eyes filling with tears.

Wanting to break the emotions and stretch my stiff tight legs, I walked to the window. "Hey, the wind's calmed down a lot, and it's getting light enough to see out."

Pepper went to the front door and looked through the peephole again.

"No trampoline." She opened the door and together we stepped out onto the front porch. We could see several trees down near the road, and plenty of debris scattered up and down the street and in the yards, but overall, it could've been much worse.

We closed that door and went to the back door facing the beach even though it was some distance away. We could see roof shingles everywhere and children's toys, and new arrangements of sand dunes and paths that hadn't been there yesterday.

We walked outside and surveyed the surroundings. Pepper was lucky. I wondered how my place looked. Even though very breezy, the storm was nearly over unless we were in its eye. I breathed in the salt air and dialed Jack who said we were out of danger, but my house was in bad shape. Lexus was traumatized, but otherwise, fine. I told him I'd be over as soon as I could get there.

Pepper and I walked to the end of the driveway to decide if we could drive her car, or if I'd have to walk to my house. The chef decided she'd take a chance, so I grabbed my bag, stuffed my few things inside, and jumped into the Fiat beside her. She had a hard time cranking the car, but it finally started and we eased along.

I was anxious to see what the hurricane had done to my house and the rental car. Pepper got to the street and pulled out around a large tree limb in the road. She maneuvered around debris and made it to the first intersection where a piece of someone's roof lay.

Looking toward the ocean, we couldn't see a street at all. It was either covered with sand from the ocean, or it had been washed out by wave surges. We looked to the right and could see nothing but naked trees, stripped of bark and leaves, and rubbish strewn across the road. Some trees crosshatched others. No cars would be going east to west. We continued across the intersection, trying not to get stuck in the sand piles.

Pepper muscled the Fiat along, grumbling about it being so low to the ground. We passed a block of houses that must have taken a direct hit or a tornado swoop. Every house had lost its roof; a couple of homes were flattened. Almost all the cars on the block had trees or a roof on top of them.

We gained two miles in forty-five minutes and we almost drove by my house, unrecognizable. Beside Jack's brick house a twisted wood frame and tons of debris had once been my old house. My rental car was nowhere in sight. Jack came to his door and motioned us in. His house, much newer than mine, and had been built to hurricane insurance specifications, with steel beams instead of wood. Pepper and I stepped inside his house and Lexus came barreling to me when she heard my voice.

"It's good to see you too, baby," I said, stroking her fur and beginning to sob.

"What a gorgeous cat!" proclaimed Pepper. "Why didn't you tell me you had a cat? She could have come with you." She scratched the furry ears. I looked up at Jack, unable to talk.

"Well," he said. "No point in telling you over the phone. Nothing you could do any how. The waves and wind did a number on that old place. I walked over with a flashlight after the wind died down. I could tell enough to know it was bad. I haven't been back. It's probably not safe. I hear groans every once in a while, which means it's going to finish collapsing. I'm sorry, Logan." We went back outside to inspect the damage.

"I'm glad you had enough sense to get out of it," Pepper interjected.

I could only whimper as I walked toward a strange heap of sand in a vacant lot near my house—my rental car.

Pepper came over and put her arm around me. "Don't worry about it. It's just stuff. You can stay with me as long as you need to. And I think we can come up with your choice of vehicles for a while." She smiled broadly, referring to one of Rick's cars.

"Oh, Pepper, I can't do that. It isn't fair to you. You've been through enough."

"I insist. And Lexus is coming with us. We'll get her a litter box, and she'll be fine."

"I think the whole beach is her litter box right now," I concluded. I gave Lexus to Pepper and took a few hesitant steps toward the demolished old house. It had been around since the early fifties and had withstood many hurricanes, but never a direct hit like this. I had a few personal items I'd miss, but I was relieved most of my mother's things had already been moved elsewhere and that she wasn't here to see this. I looked out at the ocean tossing two of the deck chair cushions onto the beach only to snatch them up again.

I was safe and so was Lexus. I figured the good Lord wanted me to start over on just about everything. In that respect, Pepper and I were somewhat in the same situation. I gathered Lexus into my arms.

Then panic struck. *Daddy's clock! Where is it?* The entire wall was gone. I looked under rubble, hoping to find it intact. I called out to Pepper, who tried to salvage my clothes. "Leave it. Leave it all, Pepper. It's not worth the effort. Help me find my daddy's clock."

We started out the back to have a look and noticed the smashed deck, the steps gone. We jumped and walked a few steps toward the beach. I saw the top of the long brown wood clock, ran to it, handed the cat off to Pepper, dug out the clock, and hugged it. It seemed to be in one piece, but the wood had been soaked. I wrapped it in my arms, and Pepper helped me stand up with it. "My dad's" I uttered. I opened the glass door, miraculously unbroken, and poured out the seawater. I knew the pendulum would need immediate attention if it were to ever work again. I wiped the clock off with my shirt hem and hauled it to the Fiat.

I would come back to the shambles later with some help. We waved to Jack and I loaded Lexus into the Fiat while Pepper squeezed the clock behind us. Lexus snuggled against me, trembling and traumatized, needing the comfort only I could give her. I wasn't sure how Pepper really felt about having a cat in her condo, but she wasn't taking 'No' for an answer.

We worked our way back toward Pepper's, stopping at a Food Mart for a few items when she noticed the "Open" sign. The owners swept water out the door and piled up ruined merchandise. A few other folks surveyed the damage to their property and to the beach in general.

The local jeweler, another high school friend, stuck his hand up and waved. Pepper snatched the Fiat over to him. We told him about the clock, and he fished it from behind the seat. "The sooner I get to it, the better. This is a Seth Thomas antique. I'll fix it as good as new, Logan. I promise I'll get it dried out, and then I can get the salt and sand out of the mechanism. Give me a few days." I thanked him and we drove on in silence. We met two ATVs making their way over to the beach. I was curious about what the beach looked like near the inlet.

Lexus clung tight to my neck with velvet paws, not wanting to get out of the Fiat. I grabbed my little bag—all I had left now—and cuddled her close to my heart. I lifted my parka off the seat and headed in behind Pepper. Pepper put the litter box on the floor of the laundry room, filled it with litter, and went to the cabinet and brought down two small cut crystal bowls—one for food and one for water. Lexus continued to cling to me for a few minutes. Once I put her down, she began to sniff around her new surroundings with cautious curiosity.

I sat down on a bar stool, staring into space until my cell phone rang. It was Charlie, almost in a panic.

"Logan, I got up at dawn. Couldn't sleep. I saw your place. I was scared you were in there. I'm glad you left the beach. Your place is a damn disaster."

"Well, actually, Charlie, I didn't leave the beach, but you're right. My place is totaled. I'm staying with Pepper Ellis, Rick Teater's chef," I explained.

He said he hoped I was all right and he would see me in a day or two. I asked him if he knew a good cleanup crew, and he said several drove in from across the state, but to be sure to ask to see official verification to avoid being swindled. Charlie also said there'd been a reported sighting of Linc on the beach but he'd checked it out himself, and it had turned out to be someone else.

Pepper walked outside and picked up roof shingles. She had quite a few from her condo, but everything else seemed intact. Being on the sound rather than the beach had made an incredible difference, at least during this particular storm.

My phone rang again and I told my friend in Jacksonville the news about his rental. He said had insurance and he'd take care of getting it out and towing it in. I put my phone in my pocket and walked out toward Pepper, struggling with something in her shed. She had a generator, so we dragged it out and lifted it onto a piece of plywood. By this time we panted. She checked the gas tank, and I tried to crank it up. Neither she nor I were strong enough to pull the cord, so we decided to flag down some kind gentleman to help us. We continued to survey the damage and pick up debris while we waited.

I heard a horn and turned to see Max pull into the drive. He said he was helping folks who needed it. We pointed to the generator, and he started it. We hugged him, and Pepper went inside to plug in the freezer and refrigerator, her biggest concerns. Max stayed all afternoon, lugging the heaviest debris to the edge of the road to be picked up by the town when they could get to it. Over a sandwich, I learned Max was divorced and had a small child. I realized we hadn't really had time to have a personal conversation.

He knew more about me than I did about him. "Before your arrival, you were the topic of every conversation between Maggie and Charlie. Maggie was excited, and Charlie was a little uneasy, I think."

"Uneasy? Why?"

"Oh I think he wasn't sure how to handle an intern. He's never had one, and certainly not one from the SBI. Maybe lack of confidence on his part. I really don't know. But I'm sure he's glad you're here now. With the murder and all."

"I tell you, Max, it really upsets me that Linc got away."

"I imagine he's still around somewhere, Logan. I can almost smell him. We'll catch up with him. He'll make mistakes. I'd bet money on it." I liked Max's confidence. Charlie, Max, and I were all inexperienced in violent deaths, but maybe together we could catch this guy. Max stayed and helped us until murky shadows brought the end of daylight.

22

"My tires! My God! All four of them!" I ran out the door and down Pepper's steps to the Fiat, sitting awkwardly low in the sand. "We must have driven over some sharp debris, but I certainly didn't feel it at the time." A tearful Pepper might be right, but I thought it odd that all *four* tires were flat.

It took several days to clean up the yard and get the tires replaced. We helped an elderly lady clean up her yard, and by the end of the third day, exhaustion settled into every nook and cranny of my body. We walked back to Pepper's, speechless. Pepper motioned me to the bathroom first and she headed to the kitchen.

"Do you like chili?"

I nodded. "But Pepper—"

"Why don't you clean up while I simmer this, and then I'll jump in. The water should be warming up by now. I plugged the water pump and hot water heater into the generator. Won't a bath be wonderful? I feel so nasty."

She didn't have to beg. I was on my way. I drew a tub of warm water and poured in some bubble bath. Lexus came in, and I closed the door so we could have a little privacy. I reclined in the suds and let the silky water relax me.

How can I relax after losing my house and my car? Nevertheless, the bath water pulled some of the tension away, and the realization that I had friends and neighbors who cared about me. And Lexus pawed the bubbles so playfully I had to cackle. The laughter felt good too. I brought a soapy hand up from under the water and scratched her head. She purred as we touched heads, and she jumped off the tub edge to curl up on the plush bath mat, satisfied that I would stay put for at least a little while.

Even though I felt better physically, I was still apprehensive about not finding Linc. And Charlie seemed to be losing interest, but maybe I wasn't being fair. He had the responsibility of the whole beach, not just hunting Linc. Still I thought he should care more about finding a killer and it gnawed at me. I toweled off and wrapped the towel around my wet hair, dressed, and opened the door. The irresistible aroma of chili pulled me to the kitchen.

"What can I do to help?" Pepper motioned me to the breadbox for a long loaf of Italian bread. She apologized for not baking a fresh loaf.

"Are you completely nuts? You're a walking zombie and the purest workaholic I've ever met." I declared.

"Yeah…I must admit I'm about to fall over."

I lifted the spoon out of her hand. "It's your turn to luxuriate in suds. Go! I won't take any lip from you. I've got this covered. We'll eat later."

She let out a faint "thanks" and departed.

I found some pretty glasses and large bowls and set the table for two. From an array of linen napkins, I selected two appropriate for chili. At my house—if I had a house—they'd be paper. I could hear the water running in the bathroom, glad Pepper could relax. She couldn't go on the way she'd been going.

Too soon I could hear her coming from the bathroom. "That didn't take long."

"I needed to get out. I fell asleep as soon as I got into that warm water and almost drowned myself! I guess I'm exhausted." She sat down at the table and tied the belt to her terry robe while I ladled us each a bowl of hot chili and brought over the crusty bread. She motioned me to the refrigerator.

"Get that container with cheese, please. I grated it myself, and it's so much better than the canned stuff." I poured us some green tea I'd brewed, and we ate in silence. I'd never tasted chili like Pepper's. I didn't know how she could take the same ingredients I did and hers taste remarkably better. When we finished, I motioned her out of the kitchen, telling her I'd clean up.

Once I'd completed the task and walked out into the living room, Pepper was sound asleep on the sofa. I crashed into my usual chair and Lexus bounded into my lap for a good scrunching. I watched the news coverage of the aftermath of the hurricane, compliments of the generator outside the window. Some areas got hit worse than others, but fortunately there were no deaths with this storm.

I yawned as the phone rang. Pepper sprang up and ran to it. I could only hear her side of the conversation. It had to be the executor of Rick's estate again. Pepper ended the conversation and came back to the couch.

"That was Mr. Rhodes, the estate attorney. He has to find someone to inventory the house before I can sign the papers making everything legal. Logan, he wants to know if you'll do it as part of your internship. He's already talked to Charlie. Will you? I mean I know you have your own damage to deal with, but I'll help you any way I can if he'll let me. I trust you." Pepper handed me a piece of paper. "Mr. Rhodes wants you to call him."

"Well, gosh. I don't know. I suppose I could, but you have to know my main focus is catching Linc. I'd have to get approval from the SBI program coordinators, but I don't see any reason why I can't if it's all right with Charlie. I know I'm required to do four hundred hours of service before I get credit from the college anyway. I can do the service hours at the police station or through an attorney's office. I need to get a car and find a place to live before I take on anything else though," I explained.

Pepper snapped her fingers. "I've got an idea. You can drive one of Rick's cars. Take your pick. I might drive one myself. My Fiat's getting old." She paused. "Well, I don't know if I could stand to drive one, but certainly you could."

I wasn't too sure about that. "No. Wait. I can't and won't do that. I think it might even be considered conflict of interest, but I appreciate your offer."

"You mean because you're an agent, and my employer and lover was murdered, possibly by me?" Pepper's tone had done a three-sixty. Where had that come from?

"What? Pepper, I thought we finished that conversation. Don't put words in my mouth," I barked at her. "I wasn't hinting around for any favors either; I wouldn't feel right driving one of his cars, anyway. Besides, it wouldn't look right for me to drive a murder victim's car while I'm investigating his murder, or any time for that matter." I rubbed my head. I was tired. Tired of having no leads, tired of storms, tired of crap, and tired of this conversation. "I think we should rest, and then we have our work cut out for us. It shouldn't take me long at my old place since most of it's ruined. I can probably pull out what's left in a few minutes. Jack says the town will bulldoze the place. I'll call Charlie and maybe his brother can help me make a decision on the inventory." The task seemed overwhelming, but I didn't want to let anybody down.

"Logan, I have another idea. While you're going through the house, which will take weeks, why don't you stay there to look after the place? I mean, if you want to. It's not that I don't want you here, but I'd feel better with it occupied."

I needed to think about that one for sure. We blew out most of the candles all over the house.

"I don't know about you, but I need some sleep. I can't make decisions when I'm this tired. And you may feel differently in the morning, Pepper. I can always get a room somewhere and find a vehicle in a few days. Let's go to bed."

"You've really been here for me, Logan. Thank you for being so wonderful. I'm so sorry you lost your house and your belongings. And I apologize for being so evil and short-tempered."

"Listen, when I think about all you've lost, my losses are insignificant," I said softly, meaning it. She squeezed my arm, and with a candle in hand, went to lock the front door while I took a flashlight to check the back door. We said 'Goodnight' and went to our bedrooms. Since I didn't have a nightgown, my panties were my only nightclothes.

***

I'd hesitated to get into bed, dreading another nightmare, but I needn't have worried. I awoke in the same position I lay down in and crawled out from under the sheet, stretched, and breathed deeply, feeling rested for the first time in a long time. I fumbled into clothes and crept toward the kitchen.

I found some individual coffee packs and decided to heat some water on the gas stove. I pilfered through the cabinet looking for something to satisfy my hunger. Pepper always had the shelves well stocked, so I had an array of choices that were nonperishable.

"What are we having for breakfast?" a sleepy voice asked from the other room.

"My best efforts with toaster pastry."

Pepper yawned, walked into the kitchen and looked out the sink window. She got two mugs and poured us both coffee. "Cream? Sugar?" I nodded to both. I assembled foil tents around two sets of toaster pastries and set them atop the steaming leftover water to warm.

"You improvise well. You're a survivor, for sure," exclaimed Pepper. We devoured our pastries in record time. We sat for a few minutes, both wishing out loud the power would come back on so we could get things back in order here, at what remained of my place, and at the mansion.

"Now we need to make a plan for the rest of the day. Your thoughts?"

"Gosh, I think I need another cup of coffee before my brain gets in gear," I decided, getting up and grabbing pot. Pepper stuck her mug out for a refill too.

Once we'd finished off the last crumbs of pastry and plenty of caffeine, I started. "I have to get back to work looking for Linc. If he's still on the beach, he might have gone back to his house during the hurricane, when we were all hunkered down. He'd be stirring around by now. But I have to say I don't feel comfortable driving one of Rick's cars—"

"*My* cars," corrected Pepper. "I didn't fall asleep fast. I feel more grounded now for some reason. And I think that's because of you, Logan. You've been wonderful, compassionate, and you didn't even know me. For a while you even thought maybe *I* did it." I opened my mouth to speak. Pepper waved her hand at me.

"Let me finish. Even though you may have thought I was suspect, you were always compassionate. You made me come to grips with the whole sordid ordeal. I can never repay you for what you've done. I lost Rick, but I hope we can be friends; maybe you're the sister I never had. I want to help you get back on your feet. I want to say thank you for all you've done for me. Please let me. Don't shut me out. I want us to be friends," Pepper said. "While you're hunting down the killer, you still need a place to live and something decent to drive."

"I wouldn't believe you were capable of murder even though some of the evidence pointed to you for a while. Once I was around you a couple of times, it was obvious that you loved the man and were devastated by his death. And I talked with Mr. Rhodes. Did he tell you?"

"No."

"I asked about your relationship with Rick and about your being the beneficiary. He said Rick wanted to make you the beneficiary and he—Mr. Rhodes—tried to talk him out of it. He said Rick couldn't talk about anything but you, that he intended to marry you and start a family. So Mr. Rhodes drew up the paperwork. He also said he did a criminal background check on you without telling Rick. He's confident you wouldn't have killed Rick just to get the estate and that you really loved Rick very much."

"Yeah," she said softly.

The ring of my cell made both of us jump. It was an excited Charlie. "Logan, the power is back on over at the golf course and Linc's house is on fire. Ned said he could hear a man screaming. You coming?"

Pepper threw me her car keys. I drove the car with four brand new tires inch by frustrating inch through debris to Linc's house where fire trucks and Charlie's police car were on the scene. Treated flat fabric tubes engorged with water in an attempt to put out the flaming house. I ran to Charlie. He said the fire was too hot for firemen to enter, and they felt certain the man—presumed to be Lincoln Tumu—was dead, since the screams had subsided.

Charlie, Ned, and I waited with many other spectators for the fire to burn itself out. Firemen kept the yard soaked in order to contain the fire and avoid damage to the golf course. The old house had been a tinderbox. I wondered if Linc had come back during the hurricane because he figured we wouldn't check it again, at least not until the storm had passed.

After several hours, the house caved in, and the firemen hosed it down with foam. They would locate the body, and Howie Hurt would have the gruesome task of identifying it. Relieved to end the search for Linc, I couldn't feel good about the way he died and not having the satisfaction of bringing him in.

Pepper and I picked up debris from all around the yard when I got back to her place. Since the power was restored on her street, she had asked some men to put the generator away.

I told her we thought Linc had died in a fire at his own house. We busied ourselves and didn't talk any more about it for a while, but my nerves behaved as if they'd been connected to an electrical outlet. I seriously had to get a grip.

"We have to come up with a plan of action and prioritize our cleanup efforts," Pepper started, not willing to discuss what I'd told her, which was okay with me. "Let's start at your place. We can go over to the estate later. The days will be getting short soon. We need to make the most of our time."

I agreed. Pepper went inside and put on jeans and a tank top. She found her thick-soled shoes and two pairs of heavy-duty gloves she'd bought to handle heavy hot foods. I made sure Lexus had food and water for the day, and we locked up.

We drove to my place, all electrical wires now out of the roadway and disabled. We couldn't pull into the driveway because it washed away. Pepper parked on the edge of the roadway and we walked up the sandy path. Jack waved from his yard and came over to us.

"National Guardsmen have come to help, Logan, if you let them know what you want hauled off. I hope I got most of the nails out of here so you can take a safe look around." Jack nodded at Pepper and told us to call him if we needed him. He had plenty to do around his house. I crept up the remaining piece of step and pulled Pepper behind me. We both walked around, groaning and observing for a minute. Not much to take away.

I was stunned all over again. The big outer walls were gone. Wind and seawater had its way with the entire house, leaving it a total loss. The carpet was a soggy mess. A guardsman stuck his head in and said they'd get the carpet up for me and haul it off. I didn't see the point.

A temporary landfill had been set up on the sound to dispose of things that could burn. Another would house ruined appliances. The refrigerator was sideways, and when I opened the door, I gagged and closed it. The place was history.

The hurricane's fury had done its damage on all the older homes right on the ocean. Some entire walls still floated in the rough ocean, their remains continuing to be pounded apart. Guardsmen tried to retrieve them and somehow avoid injury at the same time.

Pepper and I headed for her car, yelling to the guardsman that we were through. I knew I didn't have anything valuable there anymore, only a few family pictures which had been destroyed, and I knew I'd have to tell my mother about the total loss. We rode a few blocks quietly. "You all right?" Pepper asked.

Amazingly I was. "I'm fine. The way I see it, it's time to start all over." Pepper and I headed over the long high bridge to the mainland and pulled into Yam's for a sandwich. It was one of the few businesses open, having been fortunate enough to have little damage. A hug batch of sweet potato fries offered a degree of comfort for both of us.

Folks had cleaned up the street near the brass TideLand sign when we got back to the beach and parked in front. Pepper got her key out and hesitated. "I do dread this. Dear Lord, give me strength," she uttered, getting out of the car.

I smiled at her, and we walked up to the big double doors together. She opened the house and ran to cut off the alarm at the other end of the first floor.

"Damn! I forgot I turned that on. But it needs to be. I mean…" Pepper stopped. We looked at each other and laughed.

I had to find ways to settle her nerves. "Okay. Mr. Rhodes says everything right down to Rick's jewelry has to be listed. I'm not even supposed to be here, but I'll busy myself in the kitchen. I'll put things in groups to make it easier and faster for you." We made sure our cell phones were on, and I walked toward the stairs while she headed for the kitchen.

I started with the master suite where Rick died, giving it more scrutiny. I noticed dried shoeprints on the hardwood floor, and froze.

I probably did that checking things before the hurricane.

I eased around the prints and headed deeper into the room.

To keep myself straight, I started at the door and moved clockwise around the room. A picture on the wall, a table, and a lamp. Next, a potted palm like the ones out by the pool and in the spa. I reached the large nightstand beside the bed. I noted the items on top, including a signet ring and an empty Rolex Oyster Perpetual Yacht-Master watchcase.

Hadn't Chyna mentioned that Linc pawned a Rolex watch? And I think she'd said something about a ring too.

I opened the drawer to gaze upon a wide array of condoms in lemon, chocolate, and strawberry, and in various textures. I'm sure my eyes bulged. I guess Rick, whatever his reputation, practiced safe sex. I decided not to note these. Too personal and not important to the inventory. No need to embarrass or upset Pepper. I wrote down everything on the bed: a mattress pad, several down pillows, and a few accent pillows. I noted that the rest of the bedding had been removed for evidence.

I settled next to the opposite nightstand and opened the drawer. Several pictures of Rick and Pepper in happy times stared back at me. I let my fingers ripple through the contents of the drawer. I found a remote and pressed the power button. The end of the huge bed hummed, and the television began to rise from the wide footboard. I mashed *Off* and it disappeared back into the bed.

I reached for a small navy velvet box. I hesitated, rubbing my fingers over the lid. I felt like an intruder but decided to open it anyway. I gasped at the biggest diamond I'd ever seen. The champagne princess-cut ring had to be at least five carats. Small diamonds pave' set down each shoulder. No doubt meant for Pepper.

How do I tell her?

I wandered around the room, even peeking out the door to make sure Pepper wasn't coming up. I tucked the ring box back where I'd found it. I wasn't sure what to do. Heaven forbid that it was stolen, or the house burned. I pulled the box back out and pushed it deep into the pocket of my jeans. I had to find the right time to give it to Pepper, surprised Linc hadn't found it. Given enough time in the mansion, he might have.

I continued to work my way around the room, writing all the descriptions as best I could in my notebook, along with how many of each item—including the white monkey lamp pointing out to sea—and making a special entry for the diamond ring. Pepper would be going through this notebook at some point, so she would find my note.

Or should I run down and hand it to her now? No. In due time, all in due time.

Once I'd finished the master bedroom, I went downstairs to check on Pepper. She had pulled out every pot, pan, dish, and cooking tool, and made piles all around her on the sprawling floor. She didn't seem to notice me as I strolled over to the refrigerator, planning to get us both some water. I opened the door as she looked up. Her eyes went past me to soggy Margarita cheesecake freezes still on the shelf. She jumped up and ran out the door with her hand over her mouth, throwing up once she reached the patio. I ran after her.

"I'm so sorry." I leaned beside her and felt like throwing up myself.

Pepper wiped her mouth and cleared her throat. "Um, how about I go for a short drive while you get rid of them?" She headed for her Fiat while I blinked in silence, now certain the ring news needed to wait until she was stronger.

When Pepper returned in about forty-five minutes, not only had I thrown out the Margaritas but also the other food in the refrigerator and freezer, all beginning to smell up the house. None worth saving, except a few beers I left on a shelf. I decided to look around for any other signs that might upset her. I checked the laundry room and the hot tub area. I really couldn't know what might upset her. Everything screamed of Rick Teater.

23

The next morning a disappointed Charlie called to say the burned body wasn't Lincoln Tumu after all, but Joey Black, the beach drunk, the same Joey Black who had shot at the helicopter. No one knew why Joey had gone into the old house, but one thing was certain—Linc was still at large. Where in hell could he be?

I dressed and left Pepper a note that I'd gone to the police station, and if she needed her car, to call me. Charlie, Max, and I talked for a while, going back over every possible scenario we could think of. Then we separated, each taking a section of the beach to comb again, leaving no seashell unturned. I talked with people who lived fairly close to the golf club as well as neighbors of Teater's. Nobody had seen or heard anything unusual. I asked Max to give me a lift to the mansion after I dropped the Fiat off for Pepper.

I spent the rest of the day at TideLand, close to exhaustion from inventorying. Pepper came late in the afternoon wearing jeans, a white tank top, and the brightest red shirt I'd ever seen, wanting me to take a break and ride out somewhere to escape all the crap for a while. It sounded good to me.

In the garage, Pepper threw me a couple of keys and she kept the others. "We need to crank up these things and make sure the batteries aren't dead." She opened the garage doors, so we wouldn't asphyxiate ourselves. I went to the Maserati and climbed into the soft camel leather seat. It started right up and purred. I decided to let it run a few minutes since it had been sitting in the garage for weeks. I heard the QX56 humming next to me.

My other key belonged to the immaculate copper Hummer. I started it up, feeling a broad smile inch across my face. Pepper stopped in front of it and watched my pleasure, then walked on, waving more keys.

She headed for the Harley. I opened the Hummer door and watched her straddle the stainless steel cycle and put the key in. She kicked the stand up and rolled it out onto the driveway. She hollered at me to shut off the other vehicles and climb on behind her. I hesitated. I'd never ridden a motorcycle, and what scared me more, I didn't think Pepper had ever driven one.

I ran to each vehicle, turning it off, and taking the keys out. I hesitantly crawled on behind her and she took off, giggling like a schoolgirl before I could argue. I clawed everything I could latch on to. Pepper made a turn and almost slung me off, so she slowed down and pulled off the road, laughing hysterically. I had to laugh too.

"Let's take this on over the bridge and find some Italian or Chinese," Pepper hollered over the engine. Before I could respond, we were off again. She drove quite well and not too fast now because neither of us wore the required helmets.

We cycled over the mile-long bridge that separated the island from the mainland, a spectacular view—much better than from a car. Suddenly I was wearing Pepper's hair and had plenty of it in my mouth. Her long locks beat me in the face, but I wasn't about to turn loose in order to remove them.

Once off the bridge and out in the countryside, Pepper sped up as I continued to clutch anything substantial. Just as I started to enjoy the ride, a huge black bull sauntered onto the road and blocked both lanes.

"Shiiiit!" we screamed. Pepper veered off the road, through the bull hole in the fence, and into the cow pasture, only coming to a stop when the front wheel hit an enormous, freshly dumped meadow muffin and turned us over. We scrambled to our feet. The Harley was covered with cow dung.

"Are you hurt, Logan?" Pepper called out, brushing herself off.

"I'm doing inventory." I checked my head, shoulders, arms, and legs just to be certain. We appeared to be shaken, but intact.

"Did you know I have a recipe for fried bull gonads?" Pepper giggled, flapping her red shirt to release some crap flecks. As I was about to respond, we heard a snort and turned to see the bull back in his pasture, his horns down, pumping the ground with his hoof.

"Oh, shit! Oh, shit!" Pepper started to run and the bull roared off behind her. I realized her bright red shirt fluttering in the breeze more than likely infuriated the bull.

"Pepper, take off your shirt! Get it off!" I yelled as she ran farther away from me. I had to wonder if the bull was furious because of the red shirt, or because he thought she was there to collect the key ingredients for her recipe. I ran to the bike, snatched it up, and raced off after them. Pepper ran, trying to get her arms out of the shirt at the same time.

As I reached her, she tossed the shirt, and I barely caught it in my fingers as I tried to keep the wobbly bike upright. The bull turned his attention toward me and I rode off shaking the shirt at him and trying to dodge muffins. He bolted after me and I drove to the far corner of the pasture where I dropped the shirt. I rocketed back and collected the trembling Pepper, who latched on to me. I glanced back to see her shirt being thrown in the air. We sped past a farmer standing at the torn fence with a bemused look on his face.

We turned into Angelo's, getting stares from everyone outside the restaurant. Behind it we found a water spigot and hose. I washed my feet and legs while Pepper scrubbed cow patty off the left knee of her jeans and the bike. We went inside to the bathroom and washed again with anti-bacterial soap, removing particles of manure from our faces and arms. There was no goat milk soap or paper towels left when we finished, but we smelled good enough to get through dinner. We didn't talk or make eye contact until we got to the booth.

"That experience gives 'bull shit' a whole new meaning," I said. Pepper laughed and I joined her. I suppose we expended a lot of pent-up frustration in the pasture and survived to joke about it.

"Pepper," I said, after we ordered some sweet tea, "I guess the ride cleared my head. I mean, why in the hell am I writing down every inventory item? This could take weeks! I can do the same thing with my PDA. It takes pictures and I can also write notes," I explained.

"That's a good idea. Uh, by the way, Logan, I…I have a favor to ask," Pepper began.

"If it involves riding a motorcycle, I'm saying 'No'." We giggled again.

"I want you to stay in the house for a while—not mine, but TideLand. Well, I guess it's mine too, but I mean, I know you need a place to live, and I'd feel better having you there. Not that I don't want you at my condo… I'm making a mess of this."

I looked at her for long moment. "I really don't know. You should think this through. I'm fine, Pepper. I'll start looking for a place tomorrow. Really. It's okay."

"Oh, Logan. I've hurt your feelings. You misunderstand. You've been wonderful. I want you to know how much I appreciate you. I've done some soul-searching and I feel Rick guiding me in this. Even though I can't live there, you can. I wouldn't have to sell it for a while. I could take my time and not rush.

"Would you please consider doing it for me, as a favor? You could change anything that doesn't suit you. Once we get the inventory done and all the papers signed, I'll hire folks to take care of it." The waitress arrived and I ordered chicken Parmesan and Pepper wanted shrimp Alfredo. Neither of us ordered beef.

"What about Lexus? I know that sounds silly…but I'm quite attached to her, and I don't—"

"It's fine for her to move in too. She's beautiful and intelligent. I know you love her, and she worships you." She smiled. "So, it's settled."

I wasn't so sure. We engaged in small talk, not mentioning the houses, the storm, the fire, Lincoln Tumu, or Rick Teater. Our food arrived and we ate silently. When we boarded the Harley and headed back to the estate, we gave the bull an emphatic covey of birds gesture as we passed and let the briny breeze and sun warm our faces as we motored over the long bridge and back to the estate.

We pulled under the garage and dismounted.

"Got the keys to these babies?" Pepper asked with renewed enthusiasm. I tossed keys to her.

"You're keeping the Hummer, by the way," she added, walking away from me.

I ran to catch up with her. "Are you insane? You can't give me the Hummer. That's ludicrous! I won't take it!"

Pepper stopped in her tracks. "You're refusing my gift?" Her ugly tone of voice caught me off guard.

"P...Pepper, listen to yourself. You're tired. You can't start giving stuff away impulsively."

"And why not? It's my house, my Hummer, and my money, or at least they all will be in a few days. Mr. Rhodes says he trusts me and isn't concerned about me doing anything unethical. If I want to give the whole damn lot of it away, I can," she screamed at me, getting close enough to my face for me to feel the heat of her breath.

"Logan, your car is totaled. You have to have another one. Why make payments when you can have the Hummer? You're in the SBI. It suits you. I don't want to discuss it anymore. Remember, I'm a multi-millionaire, and I can be eccentric if I want to be!"

Pepper, somewhere between comedy and hysteria, ran back through the hall, shrieking. I ran after her and almost caught up with her when she jumped into the pool, clothes and all.

Oh for the love of Pete! She's gone nuts.

She bobbed around, pulled her legs up and threw her shoes one at the time at me, soaking my shirt. She started to laugh, and I joined in.

"Oh what the hell?" I yelled, and kicked off my shoes, threw my glasses on a chair, and dove in. "Damn! What a day! Wow! Does this ever feel good! Have we both gone crazy?"

We bobbed and splashed around, giggling for a few minutes, until exhaustion hit hard. We managed to pull ourselves out of opposite sides of the pool and walk around to meet near the arbor. We hugged. Pepper started crying and wouldn't let me go. My eyes filled with tears too. I couldn't imagine what this person had been going through, but I sure did like her, better than any friend I'd ever had.

"Okay, you win," I conceded. "You'd make a damn good lawyer. You realize I'm going to be talked about unmercifully."

"Who gives a shit?" Pepper snorted. "Think of it as payment for a job well done. Anyway, you can probably drive it for the rest of your life. It's huge and powerful. It'll take you anywhere you have to go to capture villains—over the dunes, through the woods, to the mountains, you name it."

"Oh my God!" I yelled, jumping up and down and causing Pepper to erupt into laughter.

"Let's get a good night's sleep at my place. You and Lexus can move in here tomorrow."

I reminded her I would only stay in the mansion until she could make other plans. She agreed. I knew I had to get busy with my PDA on the rest of the inventory. Pepper said she would keep the Infiniti for catering and sell the Maserati, Bentley, and Harley. We locked up, set the alarm, and drove back to the condo.

24

I couldn't get too excited about the Hummer since I felt guilty for accepting it, but I slept well again. I stirred in the morning light as the smell of perking coffee and sizzling sausage hit my nostrils. I yawned and turned to pick up my wristwatch. Ten o'clock. No wonder Pepper was in the kitchen. I hopped up with a groan and threw on the robe she'd loaned me and followed the aroma of sausage.

"Well, sleepy head, I don't have to ask how you slept."

I poured us both a cup of coffee and took them to the table. "What can I do to help?"

Pepper motioned me to the dish cabinet as the phone rang. She'd drained the sausage, so I gathered items to set the table while she went to answer it. I could hear enough to know it was Mr. Rhodes again. When she returned, she said she needed to meet with him about Teater Pool and Spa International. I told her not to worry; I'd go back to the estate and work on the inventory.

"I asked him about using the PDA. He said that would be great, and you could teach him how to use one. I hate to leave you with that whole place though, Logan. We haven't gotten far."

"Don't worry about the mansion. If I'm going to move in, I can handle it, given enough time. You technically shouldn't be involved anyway. You go ahead with your stuff. I can work with Charlie during the day and inventory at night if I have to. Even though Charlie said I could take a few days off to deal with my car and house, we're still after Linc, and I don't want to be left out of anything that develops at the police station."

We got the French toast and sausage on the table. Pepper poured the blueberry syrup she'd made from fresh berries earlier in the summer and sprinkled on the powdered sugar.

She was about to insert a mint leaf when I motioned her away. "Pretty," I said, "but I'll toss it to the side. Don't waste it." She shrugged, placing the leaf on her French toast instead. We ate the whole batch, and enjoyed several cups of coffee, discussing our plan: Pepper would take Lexus and me, along with my few things, to the estate. She would give me the alarm codes and go to her meeting with Mr. Rhodes. We would keep in touch by phone.

I pulled on my dried jeans and a fresh shirt, gathered up my personal belongings, checked my PDA and cell phone, and packed up the litter box and cat food. Lexus wasn't too thrilled about being uprooted again, but I knew she would adjust to the new palace and enjoy roaming around. I would have quite an adjustment to make myself. I'd been driving a ten-year-old Beemer and living in an old house. Moving into TideLand and driving a Hummer would be quite a change indeed.

We piled into the car and drove to the estate. Pepper pulled up near the garage. While I gathered Lexus into my arms, Pepper unlocked and turned off the alarm. I put the cat down once I stepped inside the house. She had no front claws, so I couldn't take the chance of letting her roam the yard. She slinked around, not feeling at all secure, coming quickly back to my ankles at every unfamiliar sound and shadow.

I closed the door and ran back to get my things from the car. One armload did it. That was all I had left. One armload. I returned to find Lexus in Pepper's arms. "Well, I turn my back for one minute and you find yourself another mistress," I teased, stroking Lexus' ears. She came to me, purring and more relaxed.

Pepper handed me the alarm codes and the Hummer keys. "I know there's nothing here to eat. Do you want me to stock the fridge for you, or would you rather pick your own food?" I told her I'd buy my own things, and thanked her again. I waved as she drove away.

I would sleep in the green bedroom downstairs near the kitchen; I didn't feel comfortable being upstairs in or even near the master suite. I placed my personal things in the bedroom and put my toiletries in the adjacent bathroom. I found a good place for the litter box, went to the massive kitchen and fixed a place for her food and water, and threw some dirty clothes in the laundry room to wash later.

I walked around the entire downstairs, ending up at the door with the broken window pane. I needed to call someone to fix it before more rain came. It had been left unattended for too long and made the mansion and everything in it vulnerable. I dialed the number of a carpenter who lived at the north end of the beach and left a message to fix the window as soon as possible.

25

When Pepper got back to her condo, she called in a panic, saying her favorite thong was missing, the expensive purple lace one Rick had bought her for his birthday in the spring. She kept it in a special box, and the condo had been locked. I told her to check again, that with all the excitement and having a roommate and a cat, she may have misplaced it.

"But Logan, one of the red Enzos I wore yesterday is gone too. There's one shoe sitting here by itself. Something's not right. I'm *positive* I locked up. That's when I decided to look around to see if anything else was gone."

I remembered the four flat tires and wondered how this could all be coincidence. It sounded too much like a fetish robbery, the kind people do to let a victim know they can get into the house any time they want, to take whatever they want, either as a tease or as a threat. I kept these thoughts to myself, and I didn't run over there. Pepper would have to deal with it. I had all I could handle.

Before I tackled more inventory, I wanted to check out something that had been eating away at me. We'd never found Linc's Jeep. If it were not still on the beach somewhere, we would probably never see Lincoln Tumu again. I wondered if we'd checked everywhere. Vacant homes and businesses and plenty of abandoned buildings were the norm after Labor Day. I had to do some more prowling around; I'd missed something. I called Charlie, and he said he was following up on some leads, and he too felt sure Linc was around somewhere. I told him I'd stay in touch.

Picking up my revolver, I made sure I had plenty of ammo, strapped on my ankle pocket, locked up, and got into the copper tank, thankfully filled with gas. I decided to start at the south end of the beach and look everywhere I thought might have been overlooked. The first few blocks were all businesses that close after Labor Day and don't reopen until after Easter. I peeked in windows and tried all doors. Everything was secure.

I moved on up the beach to several residences and did the same routine. I spoke to a lady who jogged five miles a day and asked her to call if she saw anything suspicious. I gave her a description of Tumu and his Jeep.

I went through an area well populated year round and drove down some narrow streets, making sure I didn't miss anything. I followed this pattern for over two hours, finally arriving at the hotdog stand near the only highway to the mainland.

I stopped and ordered a slaw dog and a Pepsi. The slaw dog tasted like a dried up toadstool. I spit it out, my eyes coming up to focus on the abandoned garage across the road, so dilapidated that the old grungy glass door was crooked on its track, and part of the roof looked as though it could cave in any second. I walked over.

Peeking around the edge of the raggedy garage door, I came to a halt. I took the napkin I still held and wiped away the greenish scum stuck to the big rotting door. I leaned into the smudgy glass and focused my eyes. I wiped some more. I looked again, blinking. Linc's Jeep! Pulling my gun,

I circled the old building before kicking in a side door and starting to enter.

"This is the SBI. Come out with your hands up!" I yelled. The roof made a terrible moan and released filthy debris. I jumped back, not willing to take another step in that direction.

I eased around the entire building, looking for shoe prints, listening for any sign of human life nearby. I called Charlie, and when he arrived we walked around the perimeter with our guns drawn, hoping Linc would come out and we wouldn't have to enter the dilapidated garage.

"Linc, if you're in there, you better come on out now." I got no response.

"He's probably long gone, Logan. He could get around better without the Jeep. He's probably in Virginia or somewhere like that by now." Charlie called Rick Casada to bring his wrecker to confiscate the Jeep for evidence. I stared at the building for a long time, but I couldn't make Lincoln Tumu materialize.

26

Back at TideLand, I reached into my duffel bag and dug out my PDA, making sure it still worked. I scrunched soft furry cat ears and headed upstairs to continue inventory. A rotten smell hit my nose. Perhaps an animal crawled under the mansion during the hurricane and died. I looked around and checked vents near the floor. I simply couldn't find the source.

I needed to finish the master bath and then tackle Rick's office. Rick obviously spent a great deal of time in both. While I inventoried, I would pay particular attention to finding the culprit responsible for the strong smell, maybe a sea turtle or rotting jellyfish the ocean had spewed out. Something caught underneath the house, near a vent, or possibly a torn duct into which a creature crawled and got trapped.

The master bath didn't take long to inventory since most items were permanent fixtures. I surveyed the linen closet, and found a tube of body chocolate which I quickly returned to its place. I'd missed many interesting facets of adulthood. At twenty-five I felt so inexperienced when it came to romance. I'd never dated much after a date rape in high school. I wouldn't even let a boy kiss me. I didn't think I'd ever get over it. And no one knew, not my parents, not my best friend, nobody. But now I could defend myself, and it would never happen to me again.

I fed the inventory data into my PDA and closed the door on my way across the hall. I opened the door to the office, and the rotten flowers still on the floor, caught my breath. I had found the bad smell. I gathered up what I could in my hands and took the rot to the nearby trashcan. I picked up the vase and set it back on the table. I'd forgotten about them after my encounter with Linc. A dried green stain on the Oriental rug reeked from the decay. Stain and odor had dried into the fibers and it would more than likely be tossed. I didn't know flowers could smell so bad.

Once I cleaned up the last of the decayed flowers and a few stray candy wrappers from the floor, I headed for the large desk, walking around to the large leather executive chair in the middle. I stopped in my tracks. Several drawers had been rifled. A chill ran through me.

Is he back? I needed to go over the house again. I flew down the stairs, relieved my revolver was still in my duffel bag.

I called Charlie and whispered when he answered, "I think Linc or somebody's been here, or is still here. Can you come?" Charlie said to meet him at the front door.

I stood at the door this time, waiting for him to arrive. Together we went through every room, opening closet doors, looking under tables and beds, pulling back each curtain. We finished the downstairs and moved up the staircase together. At the top we motioned to each other, and again checked every room and closet. We walked into the library and looked behind all curtains and the piano. Nothing.

We went back to Rick's office, and I told Charlie about the spilled, rotted flowers and showed him the desk drawers.

"Well, it's obvious somebody's been here, but apparently he's gone now. If it *was* Linc, I wonder what he was looking for in here again? What was worth the risk of coming back? Something to hock, maybe?" Charlie coughed. "Don't stay in the house unless you get that door pane fixed, and set the alarm, young lady. And for Christ's sake, get that damn smell out of here!" I promised him I would.

As he turned, so did his demeanor. He whirled back toward me. "Listen Logan, honey, I think I'll spend the night here…with you. To protect you. He had a knife at your throat. He might try again."

"Thanks, but I'll be fine, Charlie."

He rubbed my back before I moved away.

"Uh, no thanks, Charlie. I can take care of myself. I have guns and I'll be ready next time," I said emphatically.

"Are you sure? I'd be glad to stay with you any time." His grin gave me the creeps. "We need to get to know each other better, don't you think?" He leaned toward me.

Appalled and repulsed by his behavior, I quickly walked to the door, slamming it back against the wall so he had plenty of room to get the Hell out.

"You're definitely not staying, Charlie. We work on a professional level, and that's all it'll ever be."

He tossed back a belly laugh and walked out. I dead bolted the door behind him. I called Pepper and told her about the bad smell and stain on the Oriental rug. I also told her that unless the door was fixed I'd like to stay at the condo. I didn't tell her the police chief had made a pass at me, adding to my jitters.

"I don't want to put you in danger. Come on over. And don't worry about the rug. And I have no idea what's in that desk. I never went near it. Maybe that's something Mr. Rhodes can handle. I can go through cabinets and drawers when I feel stronger." That was music to my ears.

27

The first night at TideLand was unforgettable. After the carpenter came and put a new windowpane in the door, I decided to close the garage, set the alarm, and crash on the raspberry leather couch. I couldn't remember when I'd been so tired. I was still a little tense but satisfied I was alone in the house and secure with the alarm and my weapons. Nobody would be able to get in without setting it off, and I had a loaded gun right beside me.

There was a remote control on the table, but I didn't see a TV anywhere. I pressed the power button and the wall between two potted plants lifted up to reveal a huge plasma screen, beginning to focus on a golf match. I watched for a few seconds as Tiger Woods, on his knees, hit a nice shot from under a tree limb. It landed about two inches from the cup. So he was making a comeback after the very public news broke about his fourteen or so mistresses.

I flipped to *As Good As It Gets*, a movie I'd seen many times, but still loved. Lexus and I settled into the movie, ready to enjoy Jack Nicholson and Helen Hunt all over again. After it ended, I walked into the kitchen to find a snack. I hadn't eaten in hours, and remembered I hadn't been to the grocery store. Of course, the store was closed now, so I would have to make do with any morsel I could find. I opened many cabinets and didn't find any food that didn't require preparation time. I decided to forget it and went into the bathroom downstairs.

This bathroom was light, airy, and entirely white. A soak in the whirlpool tub would help me relax and sleep in this huge house alone. I reached over the tub step and adjusted the water temperature before turning on the jets.

I began to peel off my clothes, plunging my hand into my jeans pocket to retrieve Pepper's ring. I felt nothing. I checked the other side pocket. Nothing!

Oh, my God! Where the hell is it?

I patted myself down. I jerked up my top, shaking it violently. I looked around the floor in case I'd somehow dropped it on the shaggy rug. No ring! Severe nausea hit hard. I turned off the whirlpool, put my clothes back on, and searched every possible place the ring might be hiding. After all, it was in a blue velvet case.

"Shit!" I said aloud. This was no costume jewelry, for Christ's sake; a five-carat diamond! What had I done with it?

The more territory I covered without finding it, the more panic set in. I went back to the couch and checked the cushions, under it, and behind it. I got down on my knees and ran my hands all through the white shaggy rug. I went back into the kitchen and got down on my knees, looking across the long floor in all directions.

I sat down on the kitchen floor, overcome with shock and an array of other emotions.

How can I tell Pepper I lost the ring Rick planned to give her?

It would finish breaking her heart. I sat there unable to stop the tears that came. I'd never felt as sick or as miserable. I sobbed until drained.

Once I composed myself, I began the long task ahead of me. Running upstairs and down the hall to the master suite, I threw open the door and ran inside, already knowing the ring wouldn't be in the drawer where I had discovered it. I frantically began covering every inch of the room and continued through most of the night to search the mansion, every nook and cranny.

Once the adrenalin evaporated, I fell across the bed, numb. I lay there staring at the ceiling, wishing it would open and suck me out of this real-life nightmare. The rest of the night was eternally long.

The sun came up while I showered. Dressing quickly, I grabbed the Hummer keys and went out the back door. I backed out onto the driveway and went back inside the garage where I lay down on the cement to look across the entire garage in every direction.

28

Finding no trace of a ring, I opened the doors on the Infiniti and convertible, running my hands across and down into every possible crevice.

I glanced over at the Harley, reminded that Pepper and I rode it to the restaurant on the mainland. I climbed up into the Hummer. Retracing our Harley path, I stopped near the spot where Pepper had pulled off the road. I walked around with my face down, paying no attention to cars and trucks honking at me. I found nothing. I drove over the bridge to the mainland and walked through the cow pasture trying to avoid cow patties. I drew my gun in case the bull wanted to engage in recreation.

I pulled up to a closed Angelo's because it was seven o'clock and they didn't open until eight o'clock. I got out and banged on the door until my knuckles were bruised. As I turned back toward the Hummer, an old Buick drove into the lot and went behind the restaurant.

I drove around the back to catch the owner unlocking for the day. I told him I had lost a ring and he allowed me to come inside and look around. I went to the booth Pepper and I had sat in. Nothing. The owner and I checked every table and booth, the floor, and counters too. No ring. I gave him my phone number in case he found it. He wished me luck.

Feeling whipped, I beat the steering wheel with my sore hands, and drove back to TideLand. I tried to piece together what had happened from the time I found the ring until I realized I didn't have it so I could explain it to Pepper. Nausea struck again.

I walked out the back door, through the arbor, and around the pool, Lexus following at my heels for her first adventure outside. I went around the gazebo and down the path to the beach. Lexus sat on the top step and watched me. I kicked sand and used some curse words I'd never used before. Pepper would never forgive me for this. I walked until I could barely stand up, and decided to turn back. My stagger became a jog to burn off the emotional pressure choking me. I reached the steps, panting for breath, and sat down on the bottom one, feeling numb but resolving to confess to Pepper.

I climbed the wooden path up to where Lexus had been. I walked to the gazebo and saw her by the pool, swishing her tail. *What now?* I walked over to the pool, expecting a snake or some other rodent in it. Nothing caught my eye. I walked on past Lexus and headed for the arbor. I looked back and she was still there, mesmerized by the sparkling blue water. I called to her, but she paid no attention.

I headed inside to fix myself a stiff drink. I drank the first shot of tequila straight, and roared as I twirled around the kitchen in anguish. I poured myself another shot and downed it, letting it burn me from the inside out. My eyes filled with tears I let drip down my cheeks, wetting my shirt. I'd never felt so miserable.

I continued to drink, one shot after another. Thoughts of carelessness became thoughts of nothing in particular, and then thoughts of meaningless jumble. I didn't even feel anymore.

29

Water up my nose! I'm drowning!
Pepper yelled over me, her eyes wild and scared, her hands holding an empty pitcher.

"Wh…what?" I muttered something and she helped me up from the floor and onto a nearby bench.

"I'd say you'll have a nasty hangover, but why Logan? You passed out!"

I held my head as I spilled my guts, confessing I'd found the diamond and then lost it. I began to cry as Pepper looked equally distraught. We sat a while with my head on her shoulder. When she'd had enough of my pity party, she snatched my head up.

"You're taking a shower. You stink. Call me when you're sober." Pepper walked out and slammed the door loud enough for echoes to bounce inside my hurting brain.

I showered, a long soapy one with lots of shower gel. I washed my hair gingerly so as not to make my head hurt worse. *What a screw up I am.* My eyes were burdened by tears heavy enough to run down my face; yet they didn't.

I could hear a cat meowing. Had I left her outside? Had something hurt her? I threw on a bathrobe and went to the door to call Lexus inside. She circled my legs and meowed, but she still wouldn't come inside. She had to be hungry but went back to the edge of the pool. I decided to take another look. I walked over to her and sat down on the edge of the pool, stroking her fur. As I wiped my eyes, they began to focus on the area that held her attention.

At the other end of the pool, on the bottom, a sparkle of light changed as the water moved it. The ring! I threw off the robe and jumped in, swimming frantically to the sparkle. I dove to the bottom of the pool and pulled it off the filter grill, surfaced, and studied it, still intact. I began to laugh, clutching it in my hand. I dove again and found the remains of the velvet ring box disintegrating in the water.

The velvet box had been in my jeans when I dove in behind Pepper. Apparently the dive jarred it out of my pocket and the ring out of the box. I pulled myself out of the pool and dried off the ring. I put it on my middle finger and picked up Lexus, giving her kiss after kiss until she tired of me and scampered into the house. This had literally been a sobering experience.

I sat down hard and naked on the wood bench running the length of the pink stucco wall and put my face in my hands, not able to hold back the tears. I looked at the ring on my right hand. I had to get it to Pepper. I was no longer willing to take responsibility for this magnificent piece of jewelry, a symbol of Rick's love. My hands trembled as I dialed Pepper's cell phone.

"I'm glad you've sobered up," Pepper said before I could speak. "I'm selling the business, but Mr. Rhodes says I should stay on the board with controlling interest. I'll tell you about it later."

"Pepper, we've got to talk. It can't wait." I blurted out.

"Logan, are you all right? I'll cook. Meet me at my place about 7:30." She hung up before I could say more. I hated when she did that. I could tell from her tone she was still pissed at me, and she had the right.

But this would be better, wouldn't it? I'd have time to compose myself and do this the right way. I'd get groceries and work on the inventory before I went over to Pepper's later.

I cringed when I saw Charlie at the Hop'n Shop meat counter at the end of an aisle. "I came in here to get a coupla steaks and spuds. My sister and her husband came for a weekend at the beach to survey the damage to their condo. They brought me a surprise date," moaned Charlie. "Now I have to entertain this strange woman—and I do mean strange—because they have other plans. Not too subtle, that's for sure." I smiled uneasily, not having anything to say to him.

"Logan, are you all right? Are you sure you want to stay in that huge place by yourself? I'll be glad to spend the night with you. I don't mean anything by it. I worry about you. I can ditch this broad," Charlie offered, leaning toward me and rubbing my back.

"Charlie, if you touch me again, I'm going to make you sing high soprano."

"Okay, okay! You certainly are touchy."

I moved away and cleared my throat. I wondered if Charlie was going through male menopause. When my Uncle Archie went through it, he got into every panty that would allow him entry.

"It's like you said, Charlie. There's no one there now, and the door's been fixed, and the alarm is set all the time. Even during the day. Pepper even has to let me know when she's coming over. I'll be fine. He wouldn't be stupid enough to break in again."

And you sure as hell aren't getting into these panties!

"I suppose you're right, but you call me if you even hear the slightest noise inside or out."

"Okay. Thanks, Charlie." I changed the subject. "I'll be back in the morning to go over the evidence against Linc, and search his Jeep. I wish to hell we could get him!" I wished him good luck with his date. He moaned miserably.

I wanted to get over to Pepper's and deal with the ring situation, but I also dreaded it because even though I'd found it, I knew how my confession had affected her. Shock. Hurt. Anger. It was my responsibility to undo the damage I'd done.

30

I headed straight for the estate and carted my groceries inside, too early to show up on Pepper's doorstep. Grabbing a box of jalapeno cheddar crackers, I walked into the living room to begin inventory while Lexus curled up on the rug to keep an eye on me.

It took several hours since I had to list plants, rugs, all the furniture, pictures on the wall, and items I thought were worth more than fifty dollars in drawers and chests. I found several issues of *Golf Digest* with full-page ads for Teater Pool and Spa International and marked my stopping place with them.

It was getting late and I wanted a relaxing bath before I went to Pepper's. I went to the laundry room to retrieve my jeans and shirt I'd thrown in the dryer earlier.

I drew my bath water, hoping this time I could actually get into the tub. I looked at the ring on my finger and decided to take it off and lay it on my underwear where I would have to notice it. I flipped on the whirlpool switch and hopped in. I soaked and relaxed for a while, trying to determine the best way to approach Pepper with the ring. The soak was wonderful, surpassed only by the freshness of totally clean clothes.

I drove the distance to Pepper's in silence. Before I rang the bell, I shoved the ring deep into my pocket again. This time I didn't intend to jump into a pool.

Pepper flung the door open and I could hear a Kenny Chesney tune in the background. "Come on in. I've got a lot to tell you."

I followed her to the kitchen. "Is that blueberries I smell?"

"Yep, blueberry cheesecake to be exact. No calories when you share it with a friend," Pepper teased. "And I made another dessert too, so you have a choice." Something else hit my nose, but I couldn't determine what it was. I walked to the kitchen double windows and looked out at the transplanted palm trees, moving happily in the sea breeze. Pepper called to me to fix us each a drink since dinner would be a little late.

"I'm selling the Maserati and the Harley as soon as you finish the inventory. I also have a buyer for the yacht. Mr. Rhodes is going to handle most of it for me. I trust him, as I told you, and Rick thought a lot of him. That's good enough for me. He's been great to let me make some decisions before everything's final."

While Pepper prepared the food in her own little world, I set the mood. Linen tablecloth over the oak table. Candles and crystal candleholders. Once I had that done, I eyed Pepper to make sure she hadn't noticed. She danced around to another Chesney song, throwing vegetables into a hot skillet.

The tablescape: china plates with gorgeous colors fired in and sterling silver from a wood chest. Hot pink linen napkins completed the look I wanted. I found matches in a drawer near the pantry and lit the candles before Pepper turned around to the island again. Her mouth flew open.

"Oh, my God! How beautiful. What's the occasion?" She looked at me while walking over to the table with all the food she'd prepared. I put ice in glasses and poured the tea. We sat down on opposite sides of the old oak table with its elegant extras. I folded my napkin in my lap and looked up. Pepper had both elbows on the table, staring at me.

"What?"

"Out with it! What's so special that you would dress up the table to such an extent?" Pepper prodded curiously.

"No, we eat first. I'm serious. Let's eat now. I'm famished." I selected a marinated filet mignon and passed the other to her. I lifted out a large spoonful of stir-fry. The potatoes looked spicy but I put a few on my plate, passing the rest to Pepper. I took two of her homemade yeast rolls, knowing they would be divine.

We ate, Pepper still giving me an occasional quizzical look. I enjoyed my food, confident everything would be all right. I prayed for the right words to keep her from losing her composure once I presented the surprise. We finished off the last of the stir-fry, and Pepper rose to take our plates. I protested until she said she'd bring desserts back with her. She returned with a three-layer greenish cake with white frosting covered with nuts.

"What is that?"

"Pistachio cake with cream cheese frosting." Pepper cut a huge piece and put it on my dessert plate. She sliced herself some. We sat for a minute, putting a forkful of cake into our mouths, moaning with pleasure. I giggled at Pepper's face, now owning a cream cheese mustache.

"What happened to the blueberry cheesecake?" I wondered aloud.

"Oh, you can have that later, Miss Piggy." We giggled more. While I ate this masterpiece, I wiggled my hand in my pocket, trying to get hold of the ring, relieved when my finger touched it.

Unable to wait any longer, I swallowed and pulled it out, getting it turned just right in my hand for its presentation. "Close your eyes. I have to give you something." I told her.

She closed her eyes as I pulled my hand out from under the table and looked it over again. "I need for you to hold out your hand."

She hesitantly did. I placed the ring in her hand and she opened her eyes, staring at it in silence. She finally backed away from the table, not making eye contact. She didn't cry; she didn't yell. "Logan, where did you find it? Is it for me? Are you sure?"

"Yes, I'm sure it's for you. I found it in the nightstand drawer beside Rick's bed—the first time, that is—in a pretty velvet box, which is another story, but yes, I'm sure it was meant for you. He had a lot of pictures of you in the same drawer. I guess he was ready to pop the question. Then I made the decision to wait until you were stronger to give it to you. I shouldn't have. That wasn't my decision to make. I'm so sorry, Pepper. I never meant to add to your pain."

Pepper walked into the living room. I wasn't sure if I should follow. I decided to clear the table unless she summoned me.

I blew out the candles before I went into the living room to check on her. She slipped the ring on her left hand and looked over at me.

"I guess this is what Rick meant when he said he wanted to have a special evening with me…that last night. Oh, Logan, it's so sad. I should be crying right now, shouldn't I? I've cried so much I don't think I can anymore. But I do think I'd like to be alone. It's okay. I'm fine. And…I'm not upset with you. You did what you thought was best. I know that."

I let myself out, glad she felt stronger and wasn't ready to gouge out my eyes with a dinner fork.

31

This nightmare was far worse than any of the others. The hand grabbed me by the throat, and I screamed, loud and often, not able to get it to release me until I writhed and twisted with all my strength. The voice said, "Don't tell nobody nothin', little darlin'." I ran from it, and thought I escaped only to have its fingers clamp over my mouth so I couldn't scream. The two long bony arms snatched me backwards, causing me to fall to the floor. I tried to stand up but it had me. I began to cry, but nobody came to save me.

When an ocean gust finally woke me, I lay on the bedroom's balcony, shrouded in a curtain, tears streaming down my face, my chest heaving as if I were having a heart attack. I began to sob in earnest, knowing I was in serious trouble. I had to get help.

Eventually I dialed Pepper to see if she was okay. She was melancholy, but staying busy with all the estate and business details. I promised her I'd finish the inventory by the weekend.

"Are you sure you're all right?" Pepper asked.

"Yeah, I think so. At least I woke up."

"Another nightmare?"

"The same one. It's getting worse each time, but I'll be okay, Pepper. I just need to stay busy." I wasn't sure I believed that. We decided to call each other every few hours for support. I sauntered into the kitchen and made a pot of coffee, adding a small amount of bourbon to it. I figured since I didn't have to rush out the door, I would calm myself and get on with the inventory. As I added the cream to my coffee, I heard my cell ring. I hurried back to the bedroom to retrieve it.

It was Charlie. "Hey, Logan. Got another lead on Linc. Can you come in and ride with me?"

I glanced at my spiked coffee and sighed. "Sure, Charlie. Where're we going?"

"Back over the same damn territory. No leads off the beach at all. My gut tells me he's still here somewhere. He's got to surface eventually. I've given his picture to almost everybody who lives or works on the beach. This time a Food Mart customer reported seeing a man hanging around the back of that grocery store. Guess he'd be pretty hungry by now," Charlie responded. "We aren't finished with this case yet, Logan, and this is *your* case. This case will get you sworn in with the agency with high marks, that's for sure." I thanked him for his confidence, and told him I'd be right over.

We interviewed the lady who made the report. She was nothing but a talking walking bag of bones with greenish blond hair. I had to wonder what hairdo would be becoming to a skeleton; green wasn't it. Her voice was thin and high-pitched with no meat at all. We showed her a picture of Lincoln Tumu.

"Well, it kinda looks like him. Same long nasty hair and all, but I'm just not sure," the woman squeaked.

"Did you see which way he went?"

She pointed down the road toward Chyna's old house, so we rode over there and looked around. As long as Linc was at large, we had to take every reported sighting seriously, even if it meant going back over the same areas multiple times.

The house was much the same as before. The door was unlocked, so we went in with guns drawn and gave the house a thorough check. It had been ransacked, so we took our time going through the small house, but if Linc had been there, he wasn't there now.

We stopped along the stretch of oceanfront homes with decks extended over the dunes to the shoreline. We looked under each one, went to Pier Three and looked under it, and stopped at the beach's only water park and walked through, searching every indention large enough to hide a person.

Back at the station we searched Linc's Jeep, looking for more evidence but found nothing useful. We each headed for our offices, and I closed the door to mine and worked on a report hanging over me. An hour later I walked into the main office, ready to head home.

Charlie's light was still on later, so I ambled to his door to say goodnight. Hastily I stopped and slid behind the doorframe so I could see him, but he couldn't see me. Charlie had peeled a huge navel orange, dropping the peels in a curvaceous pile on his desk. He examined the navel end of the orange, its inner sections. He pulled this section out of the orange, and fingered it seductively for a few minutes, massaging it, and beginning to groan. I couldn't tear my eyes away even though I knew I shouldn't watch this private moment.

Charlie licked the orange hungrily for several minutes, thrusting his tongue deeper into its flesh, then sucking until its juices were in his mouth. He then devoured the membrane with a final loud groan. I could see over his shoulder what appeared to be porn he'd pulled from his desk drawer. I backed up to my office and shut the door, holding my hand over my mouth and wondering if he had come in his pants.

32

My mission: To finish the inventory of the downstairs once I returned to the mansion. I worked hard, finishing almost everything, still thinking about the strange scene I'd witnessed at the station. By dinnertime, I was close to exhaustion but glad I could stay busy to release all my pent-up frustrations from this case and my own personal demons. I made an appointment with my family doctor, but it would be several weeks before I could see him.

I made myself a salad and poured a mug of warmed-over coffee from the pot I'd made in the morning. I didn't care that it wasn't fresh. Anything would do. I mulled over the navel orange episode. What did it mean? Had Charlie always been so obsessed with sex, or was something sinister going on? Maggie said Charlie had changed. It appeared he'd become a fruit pervert at the very least. I crashed on the couch to watch TV until I fell asleep.

The phone scared me during the night. "Logan! My condo's on fire!"

I don't even remember driving to Pepper's, but she was in the yard and at the Hummer door before I could stop. Smoke curled out the front windows and flames groped the eaves. Fire hoses blasted the condo as firemen worked their way into the foyer, bumping into Pepper's belongings and causing them to crash to the floor.

"What happened? Did you forget a burner? Is it your gas stove?"

"I...I have no idea. I don't remember leaving anything on. I've never left a burner on, Logan." We sat down on the ground, watching smoke billow as one of Pepper's neighbors wrapped a blanket around us. Pepper trembled in silence, not shedding a tear.

33

As dawn brushed light across the ocean, I tucked a light blanket around Pepper, asleep in an oversized leather recliner at TideLand. She'd refused a bed and wouldn't go upstairs, finally succumbing to sleep in the chair.

By the time I awoke a few hours later and got to the coffee pot, Mr. Rhodes appeared at the kitchen door. "Where's Pepper?" he whispered. I motioned to the living room. I poured us both some coffee and we stepped outside to talk.

"That poor girl has had a time. Is she hurt?" I assured him she was physically fine.

"Agent Hunter—"

"Logan."

"Uh, Logan. Thank you. I just came from the fire station. I checked in with my son who's a fireman. He told me they found a gas can. Not Pepper's old can in the shed, but one sitting right out in plain view. That means arson. I wanted you to know. They'll report it to Charlie, of course. I'm mighty glad the fire department is so close they got there fast, or it would be a total loss. My son said there was more smoke damage than anything else, but it'll still be a mess to clean up."

"But arson? Why would anyone want to hurt Pepper, Mr. Rhodes?"

"Well, I have no right to say this, and I have no proof either, but I'm going to say it anyway. My gut'll give me an ulcer if I don't." I was all ears and eye to eye with the attorney. "Rick Teater's maid, Akiko Higushi, worked for Rick for over six years. Since he had no family and her husband ran his Japanese company until his death, I truly believe she thought she would be the beneficiary of the whole estate."

I was stunned. The slashed tires and the thong and stolen shoe sent subtle messages, but the fire sent a message that couldn't be ignored. "Mr. Rhodes, how do you know this?"

"Kiko came to me and asked me why Rick changed his will and gave everything to Pepper instead of her. Hysterical woman, almost in a rage. I told her Rick had never considered making her beneficiary, that he'd reluctantly made his father the beneficiary at one time, until he fell in love with Pepper. He adored that woman, you know. Higushi left my office in a fury. You need to investigate. I just wanted you to know. Take care of Pepper, Logan, and watch your back too." He handed me his full cup and walked away.

The cooler morning air was welcomed, but I couldn't say it comforted me. I was glad for the break in the heat and smothering humidity, but this news added another layer of pressure to my time. I wrapped a blanket around my nightgown and dragged back into the kitchen, reaching for Ruby Red juice. I toasted a bagel and spread the strawberry cream cheese on extra thick. Then I peeked at Pepper, just stirring.

"Wanna bagel?" She shook her head and fumbled into the kitchen. "You okay?"

"Still in shock, I guess. How could I have been so stupid? I'm always the one checking behind everybody else. I've never left a stove on." She pulled back her long tangled hair.

"Coffee?" She nodded and plopped into a ladder-back chair. "Pepper, Mr. Rhodes just left. He came by to make sure you're okay and…"

She cut her eyes at me. "And?"

"And to tell me the firemen found a gas can at the condo."

"Yeah, I had one for the generator. Remember?"

"No, Pepper. Another gas can."

"What? That can't be, Logan. Why would there be another can of gas?" She was on her feet. "What are you saying? My God! Who would want me dead?" Pepper turned white.

"I don't think anyone wants you dead. But someone's trying to scare you. I intend to find out what's going on. I think, in some way, it may be connected with Rick's death." I'd said too much.

Pepper pulled on both my arms. "This Linc? This guy you can't seem to find? He did it?"

"I don't know, Pepper. Give me time to do some checking. But I want you to have someone with you at all times."

"Are you saying I'm not safe? Oh my God! I can't believe this. My whole life is one horrendous wallop after another!"

I called Marcia at the sheriff's department on the mainland and asked if she could set up protection for Pepper. I told her I'd explain later. Marcia said she and the other deputies on duty near the beach would handle it. I knew I could trust her.

"I don't need babysitting. I can take care of myself," Pepper declared.

"It's either my way, or I can't find out who did all this shit! So deal with it!" I roared at her.

Pepper blinked at me and sighed loud enough for folks in the next county to hear. She moped around the kitchen for a few minutes, garbling words under her breath.

"Pepper, I'm sorry. Listen, what can I do to help you?"

"I guess you're going to have a roommate until I can figure something out."

"Pepper, this is *your* place! I mean about the condo. What do you want to do?"

"I think I'd just like to wander through alone, Logan, and see what I can salvage from all the smoke damage. I adored that kitchen. I hope I can re-do the place."

"I do too."

34

Charlie didn't want to make a move until investigators ruled the fire arson, so I decided I'd drive to Wilmington and do a little shopping for Pepper and pick up a few things for myself. I was sick and tired of wearing the same few clothes, and I needed a break to put all the mind-boggling crap into proper perspective. I knew Marcia Grady would be nearby, in case someone else threatened Pepper. TideLand was armed, so I felt confident nobody could get in without setting off the alarm, and my cell was the first number to notify.

I headed for The Gap and bought two pairs of jeans. I drove over to Talbot's for some dressier clothes: black trousers and a red and black sweater set on sale. I bought Pepper some trousers as well, and a silvery sweater similar to one she'd lost in the fire.

Next door was a shoe store. I still had my tennis shoes and some summer sandals I'd dried out, but I'd lost my dress shoes. I bought a sassy pair with a strap that hugged my ankles, getting Pepper a pair in her size.

I started out toward the Hummer and glanced at a young man, sauntering across the parking lot. He glanced back at me and picked up his pace. I threw my bags into the Hummer and saw him walking farther out in the parking lot toward the main highway. He was on foot. He looked over his shoulder at me and began to run.

"Linc! I've got you, you sorry piece of shit!" I yelled aloud, not letting him out of my sight. I didn't know how he'd gotten off the beach, but it explained why we couldn't find him. I gunned across the parking lot as he crossed the six lanes to the Independence Mall parking lot on the other side. I sat up high enough to see his head dodging between cars, trying to get away. I smiled. Circling the long line of parked cars, I pulled the big, quiet Hummer to within feet of him before he saw me. When he made a run for it, I cut him off between cars and jumped out, putting my revolver in his face.

"Freeze!" I yelled just as I realized this wasn't Linc. He hit the asphalt hard and tossed his shoe bag toward me. I pulled him up and showed him my badge. "SBI. Who are you?"

"I ain't done nothing wrong," the guy whimpered with his hands over his head.

"Why did you keep looking over your shoulder, and why did you run from me?"

"Ma'am, I ain't never seen no Hummer like that. I was just looking at it. I thought you was after me for some reason. Honest," he quivered. I checked his bag, and he had a pair of shoes from the same store I'd shopped in, the receipt in the bag. I helped him up and brushed him off, explaining that he looked like a suspect I was after, and that I didn't mean to scare him. I offered him a ride, but he declined.

I climbed back in, beating the steering wheel with my palms until they throbbed.

35

I headed over to Greenfield Lake Retirement Facility to see my mother. Just before turning onto Lake Shore Drive, a black cat crossed in front of me. Bad luck! I reached my index finger to the windshield and made an x to eliminate any bad effects of the feline. I was superstitious by heredity. My dad always crossed out black cats, and we never ever walked under a ladder. Why take the chance?

When I entered her room on the fourth floor, I could tell Mama was upset. "Oh, Logan. I'm so glad you came by. I had some bad news today. It upset me so much." Mama never admits to being upset.

"What's wrong, Mama?" Her hands trembled. I'd never seen them tremble. She was always the strong one.

"The police were here."

"The police?"

"Yeah. I'm sure you don't remember the preacher we had when you were a toddler. He's dead, I reckon. Anyway, some people from that church are saying he molested them when they were little. Remember Klarsee and Hutch? Well, they said they just realized it was the preacher. They've been in therapy for years, I understand, with all kinds of emotional problems. I knew about that, but I didn't know it had anything to do with the preacher. I can't believe it, Logan. And the police came by to ask me how to get in touch with you. The last address they had for you was in Greenville. Hutch must have told them I live here. Anyway, I told them you wouldn't know anything about it because you were a baby, and besides, I didn't believe that nonsense anyway. The preacher was wonderful with children, especially at the Halloween carnival. He always dressed as the Grim Reaper, and all of you children seemed to love him. Mr. Teater was the ugliest, scariest thing I'd ever seen in that outfit. " Mama smiled.

"Mr. Teater? The Grim Reaper?" I yelled, running out the door, leaving my mother in total bewilderment. Rick's father was a preacher. He'd been my preacher when I was a toddler. And a goddamned child molester! The long bony hand with long fingernails must have been his, reaching for me at the Halloween carnival, telling me not to tell. My nightmare!

I ran down four flights of stairs and into the parking lot before I realized I'd left my mother frantic. I caught my breath and dialed her on my cell phone.

"Hello?"

"Mama, I'm sorry I ran out like that. I'll explain later. Please don't be concerned. I have to go. Okay?" My voice wobbled.

"Tomorrow?"

"I'll try, Mama. I love you."

The phone clicked in my ear.

Lucky no troopers were patrolling Highway 17, I couldn't see the road through my tears. I had to talk to somebody—Pepper, Max, Charlie, somebody.

I screeched into the station lot and jumped out. "Where's Max? Where's Charlie? I've got to talk to somebody now!" I yelled at Maggie. She walked around the desk and asked if I was all right. I began pacing and shaking my head.

"Charlie had a little mishap, Logan. Max drove 'im to the hospital," Maggie said with a weak giggle.

I glared at her. "Hospital? What happened? How can you laugh at that?"

"He apparently took Cialis and has had a Mr. Stiffy for over foah hours. He's in terrible pain, walking like he's got three bleedin' cahbuncles on his ass," she said, trying to contain her laughter. I snickered, and she joined in, until my laughter turned to hysteria, and I wilted to the floor in a miserable heap. Maggie, having no idea what was wrong, gathered me into her arms, cradling me while I sobbed until I was spent.

"Logan, what's wrong, dahlin'? Somethin's eatin' you alive." I shook my head, unable and unwilling to speak, as Maggie pulled the phone off the hook. "I'm callin' Peppa."

To my relief, Pepper soon arrived, found Maggie and me still on the floor, and dialed a psychiatrist to see me as an emergency. He diagnosed sleep terrors, giving me medication to help with anxiety. It might calm my nerves, but I knew I'd still have to deal with the reason behind the nightmares. After I found Linc and Akiko Higushi, or whoever the hell set the condo fire. Once again, I owed Pepper.

36

Pepper stayed with me until she was sure I wouldn't do anything foolish. I encouraged her to get back to cleaning up the condo, and I'd sleep.

"I will when I think you're okay. I do need to go through everything. It's my way of trying to deal with it. I'm going through piles of stuff I haven't looked at in years, and I've found a few keepsakes. Things I'd totally forgotten I had. I'll treasure them now like I never did before. Once I haul everything out, I think I'll have the place gutted and start again. That's the only way to get rid of the smoke smell and firemen's axe slashes in the walls anyway."

"Yeah, you're probably right about that." I shifted. "Look, Pepper, I'm strong. I'll be fine. And I draw strength from our friendship. I've always believed things happen for a reason and as they're supposed to, even if I don't understand." She smiled in agreement.

"You'll be okay if I go back to the condo for a while?"

"Yep." Pepper was perhaps the strongest person I'd ever met. I admired her determination, and felt I had to be strong for her and for myself if we were to survive all the circumstances we'd been dealt.

Pepper left and I unloaded my shopping bags on the bed, kicked off my shoes, and went down the hall to turn on some lamps and see what was in the refrigerator.

Damn! That smell hasn't gone away.

I wondered if I actually took out the trashcan once I threw the flower rot and sickening shrimp remains in it. I ran upstairs to the office door. Sure enough, I'd left the rot sitting in the hall to stink up more of the house. I grabbed the can and took it downstairs, poured it in the big dumpster outside, and closed the lid. Back inside I lit some apple cinnamon candles around the downstairs and found some vanilla bean aerosol spray to disguise the odor upstairs.

I thawed two steaks to grill on the Jenn-Air when Pepper got back. I also found baking potatoes, and I knew I still had some fresh salad ingredients.

While the steaks marinated, I curled up on the couch and dialed Charlie's number.

"Hello." Charlie's voice was weak.

"Charlie, are you all right?"

"Yeah," he grumbled. "Uh, has anyone told you what happened?"

"No," I lied.

"I threw my back out and got checked over at the hospital," he lied. "I'm on some pain medicine and won't be in for a few days. Can you and Max hold down the station?" I wondered if a navel orange was involved in this lie.

"Sure." I told him about my escapade with the young man who resembled Linc, and how bad I felt. I didn't tell him about the rest of my day.

"We all make mistakes, Logan. Don't worry about it. I'm glad you didn't shoot him," teased Charlie. I told him I planned to continue the home and business search for Linc the rest of the day.

37

Since the Cialis episode, the weird come-on to me, and the kinky with an orange, I observed Charlie's actions and listened closer than ever before. Maggie and I talked about him a few minutes at the time when we could. She'd lived on the beach most of her life and knew him when she was younger. I mentioned Charlie being upset about his sister fixing him up with a date.

"Maybe he's got a sweetie...or several," she emphasized giving me a strange look.

"Why would you say that?"

"Oi don't usually talk abuit people, 'specially the feller who writes my paycheck, but Charlie's up to somethin'. Oi have plenty of friends who gossip all day and half the night, and they tell me things. You know the old bah at the south end of the beach?" I nodded. "Oi understand from several good sources he's in the back room many toimes a week."

"The back room of a bar? What's back there? I thought that place was condemned after Hurricane Fran."

"Condemned, but apparently theah's some strange activity going on, and when my friends Maude and Freda tried to drive near it, some men stopped them and said they couldn't go any closer because it was too dangerous. Oi'm not sure, but they think it's a massage pahlah, if you know what Oi mean."

"A whore house?"

"Yeah, Logan, a whoahouse. Maybe some porn bein' filmed there too. Lots of tinny young Oriental girls go theah, probably not even old enough to drink. Gertie said she heard those young girls pork each other with foot-long wieners. Oi can't say anythin' to Charlie. He's changed so much, Oi'm afraid he's got himself in a gut full of trouble."

I thought so too. Come to think of it, I'd noticed more Orientals in this small rural beach town too. "Is Max aware of this?"

"Oi doubt it. Oi just don't know if Oi should tell 'im. One day Oi think he and Charlie are in cahoots, the next, they're avoidin' each other. Oi think Charlie sends Max on extry wild goose chases to keep him at bay," She paused. "You too, some of the toime."

I wanted to talk to Max. Soon. In private.

38

I sprinted down the beach, picking up my pace as my iPod blasted an Eagles tune in my ears. I could run farther with my favorite music vaporizing the world, so the run was not only physical but also therapeutic. My breathing settled into the rhythm of the song, and I felt at peace for a few minutes. Then I took it to the limit, running all out, before slowing to cool down.

By the time I felt vibrations in the sand too close behind me, goons were on me, one on each side, arms snatching me while a hand covered my nose with a cloth.

I came to with tied arms and legs in a small dark wobbly space. Who'd come up behind me and put the ether over my nose? How long ago? I was in a boat and it rocked. I don't do well in rocking boats. I have a tendency to throw up.

BLOCK IT OUT. Block it out. DISCIPLINE. Discipline yourself.

I took deep breaths through my nose—since my mouth was covered with duct tape—and listened intently. Nothing. No matter how much energy I expended, I couldn't hear anything but water lapping on the boat. I was tied so well I could barely even move fingers, anchored well in this cubby. I exhausted myself trying to figure out how to escape.

Voices just outside the small cabin startled me some time later. "Take this note. She'll pay millions, or the agent is shark food," the voice said.

"I wish the hell you'd talk to me before you pull these stunts. You can't let her go, you know. My God, we'll fry if we get caught." I couldn't distinguish the man's low voice but the nasty female tone was Oriental.

"Oh, baby, do this for Kiko and I blow your brain outta your pants."

Yep, it's Akiko Higushi, Teater's maid.

I'd really underestimated her. But she had an accomplice—or several. I just couldn't figure out who.

I jumped when the door to the cabin I was in suddenly opened and a flashlight blinded me. As quickly, it was dark, and the door was closed again. I hadn't been able to see who held the light. Not even an outline. I could hear walking above me and feel more rocking as the walking ceased. I listened for a long time but heard only the sound of water lapping the bottom of the swaying vessel.

It was dark as ink in octopus bowels as I snatched and twisted my wrists until I felt the rope give a little, all the encouragement I needed to wring more, working my shoulders too, until one wrist rope loosened. Thankful for tiny wrists, I worked one hand out and untied the other. I wriggled the rope off my shoulders and untied my ankles.

Peeking out the cabin window into darkness, I found myself between two yachts. I snatched the electrical tape from my mouth, giving myself a depilatory at the same time. I eased around the inside of the cabin looking for anything I could use for a weapon. My ankle pocket was empty, the pistol gone.

I tore a small piece of pipe off the cabin wall, hoping it wasn't for sewage, and rammed the door open. I got quiet and listened again, the pipe still in my hand. *I wish she would. I'd like to rip her head off!* No one came.

Easing up on deck, I peered out. At least I was in the marina, not in the middle of the Atlantic on a sinking boat. I rubbed my rope-burned wrists, and with the pipe in hand, crept out of the rocking yacht and onto the pier, tripping on a few loose planks as I ran as stealthily as possible toward the lights of the marina, many yachts down the pier. When I saw two shadows walking in my direction, I ducked into a small speedboat anchored between two yachts and disappeared under a tarp. While I hid, I made a decision to untie the rope and float out into the marina before cranking the Yamaha and heading for Max Cash's private pier.

39

I cut the engine and let the boat bump the padding around the canal pier. I jumped out and ran to the back door, banging with my fists until Max snatched it open.

"Logan, what on earth are you doing here?" He pulled me in and closed the door.

"Max, somebody grabbed me and tied me up on a boat in the marina."

"What? Who? Are you okay?"

"Yeah, I think so."

"Sit down, Logan. Start from the beginning and tell me everything that happened," he said. I looked him over and said nothing. Was Max the man on the yacht? I couldn't be sure. If he was, I wasn't any better off on shore.

"How close are you to Charlie, Max?" He looked at me for a second as though thinking how to answer.

"It's time you knew the whole story. I'll get us a beer." *Uh oh.* He returned with a pony, and I turned it up, forgetting I hadn't eaten since the previous day. Max sat across from me, maybe sensing I didn't trust him.

"I haven't been at the Genesis Beach Police Department much longer than you have, Logan. Only a coupla months.

I'm there for a reason. I met Rick Teater about five years ago and did some investigating for him. He came over to my office one day and said he wanted me to get to the bottom of some things on the beach. He managed to get me the position with Charlie when George Hope went out on disability. It worked out for me to step in. Rick just recommended me, and I filled out a few papers. Before we knew you'd be interning. When you came in…well, I was apprehensive. About our case and about what you might uncover on your own.

"We? Planted? Who are you, Max?" He pulled out his private investigator license. Official and real.

"Teater hired me to find out who's behind the drugs and porn on the beach. He was concerned it was getting out of hand and would ruin Genesis Beach. He didn't want riffraff here. He owned this place; it was like his personal paradise. Mind you, he could've lived on the French Riviera, but he preferred to be here."

"You're a dic? Teater hired you?" I sat straight up, studying his license.

"Yeah, and when he was murdered, things got complicated. I have no idea who killed him. Could be Tumu. But maybe not. Teater had his share of enemies. Some from way back. There were also some folks pissed off by his bullying them around, trying to be the law here, just because he had money. Teater…well, arrogance isn't quite it, but I liked the man. He had his theories about the porn, and even considered his maid might be involved since more Orientals were showing, more all the time. He figured she had to be behind that."

"Wait. Wait a minute, Max. I'm dizzy. Got any food? I'm starved and can't think straight." He apologized, made me a ham sandwich, and poured potato chips on a paper plate with sour cream for dipping. He set a drink beside the plate. Then he set a plastic bag beside that.

"Peanuts. Freshly boiled." I hadn't eaten those in years. I chowed down as he sat patiently.

"Let me get this straight," I said, pointing my finger at him. "Rick Teater hired you to uncover a drug and porn ring, and Charlie has no idea?"

"Right. Charlie's been kept in the dark because…well, he might be involved in some way. Not sure, but it's highly possible."

"But you're sure Akiko is involved."

"Pretty sure, yeah."

"Max," I said, pushing my empty plate away, "I'd guarantee it. She had some goons nab me and hold me for ransom. They abducted me while I was running. I saw enough of them to know they were Oriental before I passed out. She thought she could use me to make Pepper pay millions, to make up for not getting the estate. I could hear her talking to some man. I couldn't be sure of the voice, but it was familiar. I believe she did the fetish robberies at Pepper's and set the condo on fire. But I don't have one bit of proof. She didn't say anything about drugs, although she did offer sex to the man. He seemed pissed with her for grabbing me."

"Maybe we can find the proof together. We need to join forces. There's more than murder going on here. You can't do it alone, Logan, and quite frankly, neither can I." I agreed.

We made a plan: I'd go to Charlie and tell him Akiko and some goons had kidnapped me and I'd escaped. I'd get his reaction and be wary of him. And my weapons—Ruger, pistol, pepper spray—would be nearby. I'd never leave home without them. If Charlie tried to separate Max and me, we'd get together after work hours. Sleep would be extremely rare, but what else was new?

"You obviously can't go home. Nobody would think of looking for you here. I'll get you a pillow and blanket. This is a comfortable futon," he said patting the dark orange cushion. "Can we trust Pepper?" I assured him we could. That much I did know.

"I'll move that boat you borrowed back to the marina so there won't be questions."

While Max took care of that errand, I called Pepper and told her I wouldn't be home for a while. Max and I set up around-the-clock protection for her in case Akiko went after her when she discovered I was no longer a prisoner on the boat.

40

I was alert to Charlie's every gesture, every comment, and every action, glad Maggie wasn't around. Charlie didn't seem surprised to see me. He assigned Max some trivial duties that would keep him out of the office most of the day, but Max and I agreed to keep in touch somehow. I filled my cup with station coffee that usually tasted burnt, and poured one for the chief.

"Charlie, we need to talk." He looked up. "You need to know where I've been and what I've found out." I had his full attention.

"Teater's maid, Akiko Higushi, has her own business on the beach."

"You mean other than maid service?"

"Oh yeah. You know the old tavern at the south end of the beach?" Charlie's nose turned red.

"Yeah. Shut down when Hurricane Fran tore it up. Condemned property, but nobody ever bulldozed it."

"No, Charlie. It's open for business—the porn business, with what I'd guess is a meth lab on the side." The nose grew darker as his eyes pierced mine.

"How do you know all that?"

"I discovered it while checking the beach houses and property. You know, like you asked me to do." I smirked at him. "I can't believe you don't know about it."

"How long have you known about it? Who else knows?" He now stood near me.

"I just figured it out, but you're the first to know," I lied, waiting for his reaction with my hand on my weapon.

The chief looked relieved.

"Good work, Logan! I'll ride down there right now and check on it. But what makes you think the maid is involved?"

"I was attacked."

"Attacked? Whata ya mean?"

"I was running the beach, and two goons came up behind me and covered my face with an ether cloth. I woke up on a boat in the marina." Charlie stared at me.

"Who, Logan? Who'd do that to you, and why?"

"I overheard enough to know Akiko Higushi was behind it but I don't have proof. Charlie, are you close to her?" His nose was dark purple.

"No. Why would you think I'm close to her? I barely know the woman." I didn't believe him. "I have no idea where she lives, but I bet I can find out. Why would she attack you? Does she even know you?"

"Apparently she wants the money Pepper inherited from Teater and planned to use me for ransom. I managed to escape."

"By yourself?" Charlie seemed surprised I could handle myself that well.

"Yeah, by myself. By the way, I've already set up protection for Pepper Ellis, in case Akiko tries anything else. I intend to find the bitch and take care of her myself. I'd bet money she had something to do with Pepper's condo fire."

"Now, don't jump to conclusions, Logan. She's probably not that smart. Protection for Pepper? How'd you manage that without going through me?" He seemed perplexed and irritated, rummaging through papers all over his desk. I kept both eyes on his hands just in case he came up with a gun.

"I have my own connections. I wasn't trying to go around you, Charlie. I care about Pepper. I just instinctively did it. It's a done deal." He was silent for a minute.

"I'm glad you're safe." He told me he'd help me pinpoint the maid's location, but he didn't seem in any hurry to do it.

I drove through the marina, my eyes looking for goons or Akiko. Was that her yacht? Or did it belong to an accomplice? Max was checking ownership.

I headed to the south-end extension to pay more attention to the old tavern Maggie told me about. A sandy path left the road and meandered to the bar. I didn't turn into the path with my Hummer, because I would be spotted from a long distance if anyone were there. I could make out a fair number of SUVs, ATVs, and boats with my binoculars. Maggie's snitches were accurate; something was going on.

Just as I pulled into a sandy doughnut, an old junky green pickup came up beside me. I drew my gun before I recognized Max.

Max grinned. "Logan?"

"Hey. I didn't recognize the truck. Just doing my daily checks."

Max looked around for any approaching vehicles, "Where's Charlie?"

"Still at the station when I left."

"We'll talk, but we need to get outta here. I borrow a different vehicle every time I drive down. Let's meet at the Baptist church parking lot at dusk." I nodded and sped off. He circled around and followed me to a side road and split off. We weren't ready to close in just yet.

41

After Max and I analyzed the information we'd gathered, I put the pierced potatoes in the microwave, threw the meat on the grill, and mixed pasta salad and stuck it in the refrigerator. Everything had to continue as normal, so I pulled on a sweatshirt and went out the back and down the wooden path to the beach, my ankle pocket hiding a new pistol, and pepper spray in my fist. A few fishermen baited hooks while others drifted off into a mesmerized tranquility, content, whether they got a bite or not.

I walked for probably two miles, my mind filled with all that had happened over the past few weeks. I had pangs of loneliness and sadness. And frustration, so much frustration. And shame and depression, although I knew a three-year-old couldn't be responsible for what an adult did to her. While working on the murder case was just what I wanted to do, it had become one obstacle after another with nothing leading to resolution. The investigation dragged. I couldn't let it get to me. At least now I knew why I was having 'sleep terrors' as the shrink had called them. I'd always been able to overcome any obstacle, and I would this time too. But my energy was depleted.

If the SBI doesn't swear me in, what will become of me?

I sat down on a sand dune and looked out to sea, hoping an answer would wash up on shore in a bottle. I stayed there until I started getting cold, the sun having set behind me. I hopped up and shuffled back to the steps and climbed up the hill. Pepper would be home by now.

I had one more small area to inventory and that project would be finished, and not a minute too soon. Every minute was now filled with challenges—the unsolved murder case, the arson, drugs, sex, my kidnapping, and the possibility of a dirty police chief.

"Hey, you! Where've you been? What are you up to? Why didn't you come home?" Pepper blurted.

"Oh, you know, just part of the job description. We don't have a schedule." That seemed to satisfy her since she was overtaxed with her own problems. No further explanation was necessary.

"I've started dinner."

"That's great." Pepper smiled and went off to fix us both a drink, this time non-alcoholic.

"As you know, I've got an offer on the house. It's a corporation looking for a place to send its employees on vacation. Money doesn't seem to be an object. I've called and rented several storage buildings to use until I can decide what to do with what's left of my stuff. The reason I'm in a hurry is the corporation wants to buy soon, and I really don't have a problem with that. I guess we'll have to find a place to live, or maybe a temporary hotel suite. But we can stay here until the sale is final," she said.

I felt Pepper was involving me in her plans because she didn't want to abandon me. The busier she was the better; that was her rationale, but it made me woozy.

She insisted on sleeping on one of the mansion couches, not willing to take my bed or go upstairs to one of those. After midnight, she stretched out while I headed for my bed. I swallowed my medication, hoping I would never see those bony fingers again.

42

As I finished off two blueberry bagels and sipped the last drop of coffee, I heard the back door and poked my head around to watch Pepper step inside, already dressed for the day.

"Hey!" She seemed in better spirits this morning. She wore the new silver sweater set I bought her, and it fit perfectly.

"I didn't realize you were up. I've been tiptoeing around so I wouldn't wake you. It's the first time I've seen you in a sweater. Are you cold?"

"It's about fifty degrees in case you haven't stuck your nose out. You bought this for me just in time." I went to an outside door and opened it. She was right; it was cool. The late September breeze teased of fall. And I was glad since I perspired all summer. Pepper began talking about the condo, TideLand, and the dream restaurant, and said she hadn't slept much.

The phone rang and she went to answer it. I could hear her discussing the sale, so I waited for her conversation to end.

"The buyer wants TideLand right away with nothing done to it but a good cleaning. Mr. Rhodes said to get what

I want out and either sell the rest, or put it into the asking price." Pepper rubbed her brow. "Gosh, I guess I kind of hate to sell it now that the time has come. If they make the right offer, I'd better take it. Not many could afford this place in this economy. If you want some pieces, we'll get those out. And throw me the keys to the Infiniti. The Fiat goes to sell and the QX56 goes with me."

"Don't you think you're moving a little too fast, Pepper? This is so hasty. I thought you were going to take your time."

"I guess it does seem cold and hasty, but every time I come to TideLand, a little bit more of my heart breaks. You're the closest person to me through all this, but you really have no idea the pain I'm in. I want to get away from the pain. Does that make any sense?" She knew herself better than I did. I nodded in silence.

We loaded some of the things she wanted to keep into the back of the Infiniti. It suited her as much as she said the Hummer suited me. We went back inside, and she did a final check of the downstairs and outside while I showered.

She smiled as I walked into the living room where she'd piled more things, mostly bowls and linens. "Like I said, if you want anything in this place, ask. I'd rather you and I have it if we want it, rather than giving it to strangers. I can use most of this stuff now," she confessed.

"Well, I like the bedroom suite downstairs where I've been sleeping. But I'm paying for it."

Pepper turned and pointed her finger at me. "You catch that son of a bitch and we'll call it square." She hurried on. "I'm not taking anything from Rick's master suite. If you want any of that, you're welcome to it. I can't bear to even go up there."

"I think I'd like the monkey lamp," I stated. I went upstairs and got the heavy white metal lamp and brought it down to my bedroom. I set it down on the floor, the monkey pointing toward the door.

"By the way, I vacuumed the whole place yesterday, so it should be clean."

"It is. There really isn't much to do but get what we want out. I'll call a professional cleaning service to polish things up a bit before the buyer gets here. I thought I'd take the couch I've been sleeping on, and the baby grand. I don't think there's much else except maybe some more kitchen things, a few lamps and tables, and those other linens," said Pepper.

"Do me a favor. See if your friend from Jacksonville can take the Fiat for me. I realize it's old, so whatever profit he makes is his to keep." I told her that was generous of her, and I'd call him.

We talked about what the movers would take to storage. Pepper said she would supervise while I was at work. I groaned, wishing I could spend tomorrow with her instead of sitting in the grungy police office doing paperwork.

"I'll take care of finding us a temporary home." I motioned agreement. Pepper told me she knew I'd move up in law enforcement, and the SBI would want me in Raleigh near her once she opened her restaurant. We both smiled.

"Logan, I love you."

"I love you too," I echoed. Pepper glanced toward the staircase and exhaled a long, sad sigh. "I probably ought to take Rick's desk too. I could use that. I guess I need to look at it. Will you go upstairs with me?"

We climbed the stairs and when we opened the office door, the odor almost brought us to our knees.

"My God, what's in here?" Pepper yelled, covering her nose and mouth with her sleeve.

I gasped and grabbed a throw to cover my nose. "I've tried to find it, but I can't, and it seems to be getting worse!" and that was putting it mildly; Pepper and I gagged in unison.

"I'm not sure I can stand this," Pepper grunted, at Rick's desk, fumbling for some matches to light some scented candles, not far from the smelly stained rug.

"It seems like things are just spinning too fast. It's making me dizzy."

"That's the stench! I'll get the air freshener from the bathroom while you get some air in here," she said, pointing me to the long row of surfside windows. After hastily opening all windows for fresh air, we left to get sturdy boxes for items going to storage.

Once we'd aired out the place, we made a second trip upstairs.

"Not much better, Logan."

"It's unbelievable."

After spraying an entire can of strawberry cheesecake spray, Pepper sat down at the huge office desk, and stuck her head out the opened window beside mine. She handed me one of her towels, and we coughed and retched for a few minutes.

Pepper turned around to the mammoth desk. "I want this desk and the two leather chairs for my restaurant office, or maybe at my new home. And I can make good use of these pieces," Pepper said, patting a few linens, and grunting through her towel. "But this odor's got to go! Nobody will buy this place if it stinks."

She reached for a silver pen on the desk, and couldn't wrestle it out of the holder. The pen bent in half. We both heard a noise and turned to watch the huge, thick wall-to-wall bookcase separate, revealing a vault and an even stronger stench.

"Something's dead in there!" Pepper eeked and danced around in a panic.

We mustered the strength to walk to the opening. I wrapped the towel over my mouth, nose, and most of my eyes. At the opened bookcase, I looked in, my head jolting backwards as I stared at the decomposing body of my prime suspect.

The screams hurt my ears. I covered them with my hands and pressed hard. *I wish the hell Pepper would shut up!* As I waved my hand for her to stop, I realized she was gone and the screams belonged to me. I stared at the most horrible sight I'd ever seen: the decaying human carcass of Lincoln Tumu. I pried my feet from the floor and ran to the window for air. I could barely make out Pepper running full speed down the beach, her arms flailing as beachcombers turned to stare after her.

43

The sale of the mansion was postponed, and Pepper decided to move slower with her decisions, both of us staying in a Hilton penthouse until TideLand was fumigated, painted, and the office gutted and restored at enormous expense. And Pepper had financially silenced the hotel manager about having a cat with us.

There was no laughter, both of us emotionally and physically spent. We moved some of our things to the hotel and stored the rest as Pepper began to deal with the condo's renovation and make final TideLand decisions. The first night in the penthouse, Pepper and I sat up talking, crying, hugging, and even cursing. The conversation soon turned to Rick's father.

"I really didn't know Mr. Teater, Logan. All I know is Rick took him in after he got sick. I honestly don't think he would have let his dad stay at TideLand if he had any knowledge of his perversion. Rick told me enough to know they weren't close anyway. He was just doing his duty for an ailing father. Learning that his father was a child molester would have torn him apart." I nodded. I didn't blame Rick.

"You know, I remember Rick telling me his dad was a preacher, but Rick didn't seem to respect him at all. He said his dad embarrassed him in front of other children. He told me his dad got into a lot of trouble one time too. With the law. They questioned him about the murder of one of his church deacons. It seems he'd had an argument with the man right before he was murdered. Can you imagine a preacher being questioned about a murder?" I was in her face.

"Pepper, where did this murder take place? Where did Rick live when this happened?"

"Uh...I think...oh Logan! Wilmington?"

"Pepper! That's where my family lived. Mr. Teater was our pastor when my daddy's friend, Robert James, was murdered!"

"But you said the case was never solved," Pepper recalled.

What if Teater murdered Roberts James, or had him killed? Could it be possible?

We both had our demons to conquer, but time and each other's support would get us there. My next task: call Cold Case and research Robert James's murder, some forty years earlier.

Kent Poletti's SBI office put me in touch with the research department that housed boxed evidence of unsolved cases connected to North Carolina, each one labeled with the victim's name. Phoebe Merton said she'd go through Robert James's box and report directly to me. I expected it to take a week or so, but she called the next night.

"Agent Hunter, I thought you might be interested in knowing the prime suspect in the James murder."

"Yes."

"Richard Teater, Sr., a pastor. It seems he and Mr. James had a volatile argument on the street and Mr. James was shot in the head about dark the next afternoon. Mr. James drove a tool truck, and a car pulled up beside him, shot him at close range, then sped away."

"Why wasn't Mr. Teater arrested and charged?"

"There was no connection with the car or the weapon. The investigator's notes indicate no evidence to confirm Teater did it. The investigator thought Teater probably hired a hit man, but it was never proven. The case was closed after a year."

That would explain how he got away with it. A hit man. Nobody would ever suspect a preacher to hire a hit man. And Teater was smart enough to cover his tracks. A weak smile formed on my face. I knew who'd killed my daddy's friend. And I knew who'd molested innocent children for years—all under the facade of being a preacher. But somehow revelation was bittersweet and less than satisfying.

44

I wrestled with my emotions until I couldn't tolerate the pain and agony any longer. I had to have some relief. I knew what had to be done, driving to Guardian Pines Nursing Facility in Norfolk, seething all the way in silence. The building was old brick but the automatic French doors opened into an awesome lobby with a mahogany staircase and fine furnishings, complimenting a fireplace and mantle.

I asked for directions to the room and started down the long hall, surprised at how big the place was. I reached the first nurses' station and eased around several wheelchair-bound old folks.

"Hello." Only wild, confused stares responded. I walked on through a maze of walkers and motorized wheelchairs and headed toward the next nurses' station. I turned left as instructed and almost ran into a lady in some contraption that kept her upright and mobile.

"Hello."

"Nobody cares!" she hissed at me. I maneuvered around her, and guardedly approached Room 69W. Under the number was the name R. Teater. I shuddered and peeked in. The first bed was empty. Near the window sat an old man in a wheelchair, his white hair wild, his torso crumpled over the side. Anger boiled within me. I clenched my teeth and strutted in with purpose.

"Mr. Teater?" His head slowly lifted, and his glazed eyes tried to focus on me. I cleared my throat to say what I'd come to say. Then the stench hit my nose as he shifted in the chair, trying to sit up straight. He'd soiled himself and was helpless to do anything about it.

I'd driven all this way to slap him senseless and tell him to go straight to Hell only to realize he was already there. I swallowed hard, my anger dissipating, his Hell my satisfaction. I pushed the nurse's button just out of his reach.

"May I help you?"

"Mr. Teater needs some assistance," I responded in a voice unfamiliar to me. I dropped the button and walked away, never looking back.

45

I sat at my station desk listening to Charlie shuffling papers in his office, and completing page after page of the Richard Teater murder report on all the evidence I'd found, and finding Lincoln Tumu's remains. My heart was heavy, and my gut flipped over itself several times—for lots of reasons.

Max and I had spent enough time together to draw some troubling conclusions. We were certain Charlie tried to keep us from comparing too many notes that might implicate him in the beach's sordid affairs. But we needed proof.

I stopped writing and ran my fingers through my hair and down my face. How many nightmares should one person have to endure? I thought not only of myself but also Pepper. And what about Lincoln Tumu? I wondered if he'd really killed Rick or just robbed him. Maybe his greed had made him unlucky when the power outage closed the vault he was in. Or had someone else locked him in? I might never know.

Charlie stuck his head in. "Logan, I'm outta here. See you tomorrow. Lock up for me?"

I nodded and gave him a weak smile. I waited until I heard his car drive away and went to the window to follow it out of sight in the direction of the old tavern before unlocking his office door. My knotted gut prompted me to pull open each drawer of his desk. I laid aside several file folders and found a stack of blank NCR report pads. Once I lifted the pads, my eyes focused on pictures of Chyna and several very young girls, scantily clad, with Charlie. They all looked stoned. Charlie wore a big grin and little else. Akiko Higushi was draped over his shoulder. I stared. She had on a thong and no top, her small hand on Charlie's hairy chest.

I looked back through the drawer and found a thick folder with phone numbers, drug suppliers, maps to meth labs, and customers. Customers' initials were listed with phone numbers. They wouldn't be too happy about Charlie's careless arrogance.

Another folder was crammed with pre-teen Asian girls with Internet porn sites listed beside each. I held up negatives of little naked girls, some maybe as young as ten, and some with headless men spewing semen in their faces, the disgusting evidence I needed. I had to do something to stop it, and I was smart enough to know I needed back up. I dialed Max but got no answer.

I sat down in Charlie's chair and lost myself in the contents of the folders, identifying dealers and their locations, and finding several nude poses of Akiko, autographed for Charlie.

A deep sigh got my attention. I looked up to see Charlie standing in the doorway with a nine-millimeter pointed at me.

"Logan, Logan, Logan. Why couldn't you leave well enough alone?" I stood up. He slammed me back down. "Don't make any sudden moves, little girl. How'd you figure it out?" I sat there, my .38 on the desk in my office. *Shit* I was trained to hear a pin drop and yet he'd surprised me.

"Why, Charlie?"

He pushed some papers to the floor and sat on the edge of the desk, trapping me in the corner. He could see I didn't have my revolver. He snatched me out of his chair and pulled my arms behind me, slapping the cuffs on.

"Just to keep you honest, Missy. Rick found out about the drugs. In fact, he collected them from…a dealer and turned them over to me. I reckon that's called irony or just plain stupidity. Such a trusting fool, that Rick. I've known Chyna since she was a little thing. I knew Linc too, but never liked him. A cokehead. We used him in some videos, but he was so drugged he couldn't keep it up.

"Chyna…well, now there's some succulent flesh. I've had my share of her. She don't like fisting, though. She slapped me hard, and I had to rough her up a little. But those little Asian angels'll do anything to be in America. Kinky sex, blowjobs, prostitution, drug mules. You know, the land of opportunity." He grinned.

"Was Rick Teater going there for sex?"

"Hell no! He could have his delivered to the mansion, but he wasn't anything like his reputation. I think he was scared of catching something. Anyway, Rick found out about the drugs only because of my partner's stupidity. I never had anything against him. If he had minded his own business, he'd still be alive. When good ole Linc and Chyna drugged and robbed him, it was perfect. I couldn't have planned it better myself. You know how important timing is, Logan."

"So after Linc and Chyna drugged and robbed him, you went in and finished the job."

Charlie waved his arm. "No, you got that all wrong, sister. I didn't kill him. He was dead when I got there. Seriously. I just helped frame Linc."

"So Linc didn't kill him."

Charlie shook his head and grinned. "No, but you sure chased his raggedy ass to death, didn't you?"

I recoiled. "Then who did, Charlie? Who really killed Rick Teater?" He grabbed my cuffed arm. "Is Max in on this too?"

"That ass fly? Not hardly. He doesn't know his head from his asshole. Now that's enough small talk. We're getting out of here and one of us ain't coming back." Charlie dragged me out from behind his desk, and we headed for the door. I glanced back at my office desk where my revolver lay. And my .25 was out of reach with the cuffs behind my back.

I tried to twist away from the chief, a person and a half heavier, but he had a firm grip on my arm, and his pistol was close to my head. Charlie wrestled me into the back seat of his cruiser behind the cage. I'd never been in the backseat, and I didn't like it. He jumped in and raced down the dark highway, heading to the isolated north end of the island.

"Charlie, you don't want to do this. You have to know people will be looking for me."

"Yeah? Like who?" Charlie laughed. "You don't have any family here, and the only friend you got is that chef who's about out of her mind."

Where the hell is Max? Has Charlie done something to him?

"Did you burn her house? Why? What was that for?"

"I didn't have nothing to do with any of that shit! More stupidity. Jealousy and spite."

"Then Akiko did it," I yelled out. "And she had me abducted. And she's behind the porn on this beach."

"Well, aren't you the clever cunt? Kiko really should've got that mansion, Logan. She gave Teater over six years of complete loyalty, and the sanctimonious bastard fired her just because she bagged a few grams at his table and he caught her. Ass-wipe Linc and Chyna decided to rob Teater. Kiko didn't know nothing about that, but as luck would have it, they drugged him. And thick dick Linc left his socks and a nice set of deformed footprints. Piece of cake. And Chyna did exactly what I told her to do after your lame-brain interrogation."

So Rick fired the maid, and she came back later, waited for Linc and Chyna to leave, and then finished off Rick.

Charlie drove recklessly and reached beside him for his bottle of Smirnoff's courage. He guzzled it straight and didn't even flinch. I knew I wouldn't be coming back unless I came up with a plan, and tricking Charlie wouldn't be easy. No cell phone, no nothing.

If he'd just cuffed me in front. I looked around the seat, but there wasn't anything to grab and no way to reach Charlie through the cage.

"So how long you been in operation, Charlie?" I called out, my voice bouncing with the car, now on hard sand full of deep indentions.

"Shut up! Keep your flappin' mouth shut, Logan!" he growled, taking another long guzzle of vodka. "You came here and screwed up everything. But I have to tell you, I didn't give you enough credit. You actually have a brain in that skinny-ass body." Ordinarily I would have taken that statement as a compliment, but under the circumstances, I didn't feel the least bit flattered.

"So where's Kiko? Where is she now, huh? Why are you doing her dirty work, Charlie, because you're *doing* her?"

"Any fucking time I want to. Now shut the hell up!"

My heart thumped hard enough to explode even though I tried to take long slow breaths. We came to the jetty at the end of the island. He gulped two more gigantic swigs of vodka before he got out.

He dragged me from the backseat and pulled me toward the treacherous rocks barely visible in the darkness.

Still on the sand, I ran, even though the cuffs in back made me slow. Charlie chased me, cursing with every breath, and when he fell behind, he squeezed off a warning shot to stop me. I had nowhere to hide. Charlie was out of breath, but with the cuffs and his gun, he muscled me to the jetty.

The ocean—first deafening, then whispering—ebbed and flowed, the normally peaceful sound now incredibly vicious. He bullied me along the rocks, moving farther out where the waves crashed over the end with ravenous tentacles grasping for anything that might venture too close.

"Am I supposed to accidentally drown with cuffs on, Charlie? That would create some mighty interesting questions, wouldn't it?"

"Oh, yeah, I need to remove those, I s'pose. You know, I had a thing for you, Lo…gan, and you never eve notice. I like blondes, sma ones too. You and me could've be a team. Now it's come to this. Don't try nothin' stupid." The inebriated chief uncuffed me.

I figured I didn't have anything to lose. "I noticed you, Charlie, but I'm just not into drugs or kiddy porn." I moved toward him and then pretended to trip on a rock that jutted upwards, and quickly grabbed the .25 caliber from my ankle pocket.

A shot rang out. I crouched, and watched Charlie reach for his back where blood spurted as he collapsed near me. I grabbed his gun, and turned to look toward the beach, still hunkered down. Akiko Higushi ran down the uneven jetty, screaming and firing rounds at me. "No! No. Chalie. No. I no mean to hit you," she howled.

I aimed at the maid. "Drop the gun, Kiko or I'll take you out!" She kept coming with a vicious growl, about to lunge when I hugged my trigger and squeezed. The bullet caught her in the chest, dead center, and she flipped off the jetty into the ocean. I looked back to the beach and saw another figure running toward me. As I prepared to shoot, I recognized Max.

We pulled Akiko's limp body from the sea, relentlessly slamming her against the rocks. Then I noticed the blood dripping down my hand, coming from a flesh wound in my upper arm. The EMS truck Max had called arrived with sirens blaring, Charlie now wailing.

46

As Max drove me to the emergency room, he told me all his tires had been slashed, and he had to steal a car to try to catch up with us. He'd been keeping the chief under surveillance around the clock, not easy since the man seldom slept. When he saw Charlie return and put me in the cruiser, he knew I needed assistance. Akiko drove up in time to see Charlie take off with me, and followed us at a distance. Max tailed her.

"I always had your back, Logan, even if it was from a distance."

I thanked him for lending a hand. "I'm glad you agreed to take over as the Genesis Beach police chief."

"It's only temporary. I'm not really cut out for it, but I don't want to leave the beach with no law enforcement."

We called the Coast Guard and enough SBI manpower to shut down the porn and meth, and to make certain none of the culprits got away by land or by sea.

Akiko's shot paralyzed Charlie from the waist down; no more Mr. Stiffy, but he'd live. Akiko's remains would be flown home to Japan.

I was treated and discharged into Pepper's care for a few days while she postponed her other plans to see that I ate and rested. I finally experienced the marvelous, restful sleep I'd missed for so many months, soothed once again by Daddy's clock and the whisper of Genesis Beach.

About Author Susan Whitfield

Susan Whitfield is a life-long resident of North Carolina. She grew up in Pender County near Black River and now resides in Wayne County with her husband, Doyle. Whitfield published three other mystery novels, *Just North of Luck*, *Hell Swamp*, and *Sin Creek*. She also compiled recipes from mystery writers across the country for *Killer Recipes*, a cookbook with proceeds going to cancer research. Her web site includes more information:

www.susanwhitfieldonline.com

Reviews For Susan's Books

Genesis Beach

"...a spine-tingling mystery...Add the Logan Hunter series to your reading list." Lynette Hall Hampton, *Echoes of Mercy*

"...engaging characters, a tight plot and a beautiful, yet unpredictable setting. Pack this one for the beach and enjoy the first book in a promising series." Mary Fran Vesey, *Murder at Treese Family Inn*

"...holds your interest to the very end." Martha Cheves, *Stir, Laugh, Repeat*

"Whitfield crafted an enjoyable mystery filled with vibrant character, capturing the essence of coastal North Carolina." K.R. Jones, *The Ghosts of Guantanamo Bay*

Just North of Luck

"Whitfield takes the reader to the backwoods of North Carolina...[and] weaves a tale that leaves us breathless..." Sylvia Dickey Smith, *Dance on His Grave* and *Deadly Sins-Deadly Secrets*

"...eloquent descriptions of the Blue Ridge Mountains and grisly murders that take place in that beautiful setting will haunt readers." Sunny Frazier, *Fools Rush In*

"Not for the faint of heart." Mark Stevens, *Antler Dust*

"Just North of Luck grabs you by the scruff of the neck and takes you on a harrowing ride from the very beginning... The second book in the Logan Hunter series is a must read." Elise Crawford, *A Promise Kept*

"Quirky characters, humor, and a keen sense of place..." Bob Avery, *Beneath A Buried House*

"Just south of sanity!" Apex Reviews

Hell Swamp

"...a Carolina Low Country tale of greed and misguided deeds. Fasten your seat belt!" Maggie Bishop, *Murder at Blue Falls*

"...Hell Swamp is a good old-fashioned roller coaster ride. Whitfield sprinkles in humorous and colorful descriptions...enough for an occasional chuckle in a tense situation." David Fingerman, *Silent Kill*

"Hell Swamp...riveting from page one, you'll want to read with all the lights on and the doors locked." Teresa Jenner Garrido, *Wind Whisperer*

"The action in Hell Swamp jumps out at you from the first chapter and never lets up. Edgy stuff." Mary Deal, *River Bones*

"...well-written, suspenseful mystery with a likeable protagonist, vivid imagery, a taste of horror, a little tongue-in-cheek humor and even romance. What's not to like?" All Books Review

"Whitfield has drawn a cast of characters from down by the Black River...peculiar, scary and injected with just enough humor to make Hell Swamp stand out from the pack. Read the book. It's a good 'un." Tom Cooke, *Memoirs of Bear*

Sin Creek

"This action-packed mystery will keep you turning the pages until its shocking end." L.J. Sellers, *The Sex Club* and *Secrets To Die For*

"Lickety-split pace and effective description [in Sin Creek] give the reader the feeling that they are conducting the investigation right along with Logan Hunter. If you're a fan of mysteries, this one is guaranteed not to disappoint. If mystery's not your usual genre, make an exception with Sin Creek. Like the Cyclone at Coney Island, Sin Creek is gripping and intense, yet an enjoyable ride." Mark Rosendorf, *The Rasner Effect*

Killer Recipes

"Don't be afraid to try these concoctions. We only write about murder and poison, we don't participate in them." J.D. Webb, *Smudge*

"Titles are hilarious...recipes are real and delicious. Whitfield has put a fun slant on the old standard cookbook." Mary Deal, *Down To The Needle*

"I'm giving copies to friends for gifts...a worthwhile addition to my cookbook collection." Gayle Wigglesworth, *Mud To Ashes*